Virginia L. Pulitzer (signature)

Gwendolyn Claire
VS
THE FOXFIELD FOUR

By Virginia L. Pulitzer

Dedication

With love to my supportive family: husband Arthur, daughter Heather, son-in-law Andrew, and grandsons: Andrew, Colin, and Harry.

Table of Contents

Chapter 1
The New Kid Again

School started September 4ᵗʰ for all Foxfield students but me. As any kid knows, the first week of school is the most important week of the whole year. Life in school practically depends on starting class on the very first day of the very first week; that's the day that you begin to learn "survival skills." For example, in the first week of fourth grade last year I learned several crucial bits of information: that Sam Stanton brought a new stash of pencils to school every Monday and didn't mind lending them once in awhile; that all the week's leftover peas and carrots swam in Friday's soup and Wednesday's pizza was not half bad; that the nearest girls' room was in the fifth grade hall, but the fifth grade girls were vicious; that Mrs. Atkins, the music teacher, gave homework; that we had a twenty word spelling test every Friday; and, most importantly, I learned which kids were friend material and which kids were not.

Today is the 22nd of September. I am so out of it. Everyone knows the "survival skills" but me. It might as well be November. Our move took longer than we expected. Anyway, I clenched my teeth and tried to smile as Mrs. Patterlin took my hand (Yikes, I felt about 2 years old.) and led me into room 25.

I hate this part. I've moved three times already and getting introduced is so embarrassing. Everyone else already knows everyone else; especially by the time they get to 5th grade. In fact most kids have known each other since kindergarten. I am a Martian being taken by the leader to meet the strange and scary citizens of an alien planet.

"Attention, class. Could I please have everyone's attention?"

Mrs. Patterlin towered over me like the Empire State Building; boy, was she tall. Her perfume smelled extra strong on this Indian summer's day and my stomach began churning as the flowery odor mixed with the blueberry muffin from breakfast. All at once my confidence left my head, whizzed through my stomach, slid down my legs, and seeped out my toes. Eighteen heads with eighteen pairs of eyes turned at the same time to focus on my face. My insides twitched something fierce. A girl in the front had her back to Mrs. Patterlin.

"Olivia, are you with me?"

Olivia, a blonde-haired girl with crystal blue eyes and way too much lip gloss, turned slowly around in her seat and added a nineteenth pair. Olivia smiled sweetly at Mrs. Patterlin and folded her hands on her desk.

"Thank you, dear."

All eyes were now on me.

As Mrs. Patterlin directed her attention to the rest of the class, WHAM! Miss Blue Eyes stuck her tongue out at me. My mouth dropped open in amazement.

Mental note: entry #1 on my "To Be Avoided" list – Olivia, a potential problem.

"Class, I would like you to welcome a new student to our school, and, of course, to our little family here in room 25."

2

Little family? Does that mean that Olivia is my "sister?" Great. My brain hurt from the thought.

Already I felt as if I had been standing on a guillotine for hours. "Put my head on the chopping block already." I begged silently.

No luck.

Mrs. Patterlin droned on, "Class, please welcome Gwendolyn Claire. I'm sure that you will make her feel at home."

Home – that's exactly where I wanted to be.

Most of the kids just looked at me and some even smiled, but Olivia Blue Eyes just glared at me. Welcome to Foxfield Elementary, Gwendolyn Claire.

Chapter 2
Things Get Worse

Feeling totally embarrassed, I took my seat in Cluster 2 after Mrs. Patterlin gave me "special permission" to sharpen my pencils. The other kids were already used to the "Grade 5 Rules." Everywhere in the September classroom, the posted rules stared down like fiery-eyed dragons threatening to devour me with every violation. My nerves kicked into high gear and, as usual, my right eye started twitching.

"What's the matter with your eye, Gwendolyn Claire?" Olivia brayed loud enough for everyone to hear. Oh, did I tell you that Olivia, "Livi" to her friends, sat right next to me? Lucky me.

Before I had time to answer, Olivia invaded my space, stared without blinking, and pointed at my right eye. I wanted to grab and bend her finger back so bad, but I held onto my chair with white-knuckled hands and whispered through gritted teeth while looking down at my desktop. "Nothing. Nothing is the matter with my eye."

"But it's wiggling; wiggle, wiggle, wiggle," she continued waving her finger inches from my nose. "Look, Andrew, her eye is wiggling."

Andrew, a brainy-looking boy with auburn hair, wire-rimmed glasses, and a green plaid shirt, holding an eraser-less pencil about the size of his thumb, looked up from his journal writing with a "What now? Leave me alone" look on his freckled face. He did have nice brown eyes behind those thick lenses.

"Her eye, look at it. It's wiggling. Wiggle, wiggle, wiggle."

In an instant everyone in the classroom knew that my right eye was twitching like the beacon on a lighthouse during a hurricane.

Embarrassed and angry and certainly without thinking, I stood up, snatched Olivia by the ponytail and lifted her off her seat. She let out a scream so loud that Mrs. Patterlin choked on her coffee, dropped her cup on the floor, got up too quickly, slipped on the spill, and landed on her behind under her desk. With her fanny on the floor, Mrs. Patterlin's head looked bodiless and appeared to balance on her desk. A couple of kids ran over to help her up while Olivia continued bellowing like a wounded calf.

"Ow! My hair! Let go of me, you jerk! I'll get you for this!"

For some reason I couldn't let go. My hand moved her ponytail roughly back and forth in time with the rhythm of my words. "So my eye is wiggling; big deal. I suppose your eye never wiggled." Olivia's head looked like the Derek Jeter bobble-head doll I once got at a Yankees game.

Amanda, Missy and Molly (who I would later find out looked to Olivia as their leader) ran to her aid.

"Let her go; you freak." Amanda tried pulling at my arms. Of course, that only added to the tug on Olivia's hair.

What a scene, a nightmare really; I watched myself in the middle of something horrible. I had wanted to be invisible today, an observer, a fly on the wall, just kind of sit back and watch how things worked at Foxfield School. Fat chance of that happening! I could see the school newspaper's headline now: "New Kid Expelled on Her First Day at Foxfield."

Mrs. Patterlin, finally off the floor, straightened her flowery skirt and school bus yellow blouse and waddled as quickly as she could toward the madness.

Olivia, screaming at the top of her lungs, helicoptered her arms in the air and just missed my face with each revolution. By now Amanda, Missy and Molly had formed a human chain behind me. Pulling with all her might, Amanda led the chant.

"Let her go. Let her go. Let her go."

But I didn't.

My hands, with lives all their own, held the ponytail in a death grip.

The girls who didn't like Olivia cheered; guys like Andrew just watched trying not to get in trouble themselves; and the loudest and dumbest boys began applauding and jumping in place like fans watching a hockey brawl. Some great first impression I was making.

Mrs. Patterlin finally arrived and, with her large plump hands, tried to loosen my grip.

"Gwendolyn Claire, let go this very minute!" Mrs. Patterlin's face looked like a boiled tomato ready to burst.

"Go, Gwen, go!" Benny, a member of the hockey crowd, shouted with cupped hands from the back of the room.

Everyone completely lost it then and laughter erupted like a volcano.

"Benny, enough!" Mrs. Patterlin exploded.

My brain, in spite of the chaos in the room, made a mental note about Benny: Benny Something, class clown.

My grip continued to tighten, but somehow Mrs. Patterlin pried off my hands and stumbled backwards. Amanda hurried to console Olivia. I froze.

Huffing and puffing, Mrs. Patterlin managed to spit out three words with a gasp in between each, "EVERYONE (gasp) SIT (gasp) DOWN." Then she added: "Gwendolyn, you may spend the remainder of the day in the time-out desk. Get a daily note from the black tray on the work table so I may let your mother know about your incredibly unacceptable behavior this morning."

All eyes again focused on my face. The thick absolute silence in the room caused salty tears to slide down my cheeks as I followed orders like a sleepwalking robot. Olivia and Amanda drilled their eyes into

7

me and smiled nasty smiles. Everyone else just stared. I wished I were back in Hartwick Elementary. I missed my old friends and my old school. Just then I noticed that Andrew and a girl from Cluster #1 by the door were giving me warm smiles. I suddenly didn't feel so alone. The dark cloud surrounding me began to lift.

I spent the remainder of the time before gym in the time-out desk. While everyone else was finishing journal entries and morning work, I copied the "Grade 5 Rules" five times in my best handwriting.

Grade 5 Rules

1. Do not leave your seat without asking permission.
2. Raise your hand to get permission to speak.
3. Before the day begins, sharpen two pencils.
4. Keep your hands to yourself.
5. Treat others as you would like to be treated.

Boy, did I ever mess up #4. My first day at Foxfield and I get a time-out. I never received a time-out at Hartwick. Mom didn't need this kind of news. I felt like a naughty animal in the zoo. Since the time-out desk was right next to Mrs. Patterlin's desk, every time someone came up to ask a question, he or she glanced over at me.

"Mrs. Patterlin," Olivia whined as she smiled smugly at me, "I don't get # 5."

Number 5 was simple multiplication. Either Olivia was really bad at math or her question was just an excuse to get close enough to give me one of her looks.

"Livi, dear," Mrs. Patterlin answered smiling, "Look at the key word in the problem."

Olivia kept her eyes on me while answering Mrs. Patterlin.

"Oh, I get it now. Thanks, Mrs. Patterlin." As she turned to leave, Olivia made sure to throw me another miserable look. The M&M's, my name for Missy and Molly, also threw poison darts across the room. "Livi Dear" kept playing the victim all morning while gathering "you poor thing" glances from her group.

It was finally time for gym. Mrs. Patterlin rang the silver bell on her desk and, with a voice that sounded a lot like the Charlie Brown teacher on a <u>Peanuts</u> cartoon, called for line leaders.

"Could my line leaders please line up for gym? Jared? Livi, dear?"

Everyone rushed to clear desks.

I felt like Robinson Crusoe. The other side of the room seemed so far away.

Jared and "Livi Dear" took their positions of honor at the door while clusters waited to be called. I started getting nervous again. I tried hard to stay calm so my eye wouldn't twitch. Should I get up when Cluster #2 was called or should I wait to be called separately? After all, here I sat, alone and temporarily "unclustered."

"Cluster 4."

All the 4's, except for two boys, pushed in their chairs and lined up. I would later learn that the two were Ivan and Vladimir, our ESL (English as a Second Language) students, and that they sometimes worked as a "I don't understand" tag team and cleverly used their ESL label like a child with a cold takes advantage of his mother's kindness.

"Ivan, go back and push in your chair."

Almost nothing could escape "Hawk-Eye" Patterlin.

Ivan with his close-cropped blonde hair, 4' 11" height, and small body could easily maneuver the room almost without being noticed.

"Cluster 5." continued Mrs. Patterlin.

All chairs slid smoothly into place.

"Cluster 1."

Two more clusters to go and one of them was mine. Oh, no. My eye began some major twitching again.

"Cluster 3."

Cluster 3 emptied quickly.

Only Cluster 2 remained. What should I do? Should I get up when Cluster 2 was called or just stay put and wait to be remembered? I decided to play it safe and stay put. I didn't want to break yet another rule on my first day.

"And, last, but not least, Cluster 2." My cluster-mates scurried to their spots and I just sat there alone by the window with a bookcase blocking Mrs. Patterlin's view of me.

"Okay, ready class? Zip and flip."

"Zip" meant to stop talking and "flip" meant to fold arms in front of us.

The "flip" reminded me of Jeannie in <u>I Dream of Jeannie</u>; an old television show from the 60's that we watch on <u>TV Land.</u>In the show Jeannie, a bottled genie that lives with an astronaut in Florida, "flips" her arms in front of her and nods her head in order to disappear. Boy, that's exactly what I wanted to do- flip my arms, nod my head and disappear forever from room 25 and Foxfield School. Maybe I could reappear on some deserted island far away from this mess.

"Okay, let's go." Mrs. Patterlin turned to go and didn't look back.

A silent scream escaped my mind. "Wait a minute. How about me? You're leaving without me." My arms waved wildly in the air while I desperately tried to get Mrs. Patterlin's attention. Rules #1 and #2 repeated themselves over and over in my head: "Do not leave your seat without permission." AND "Raise your hand to get permission to speak." How could I speak or leave my seat without getting into deep trouble for the second time today? I felt crazy-glued to my seat.

Olivia was the last one to leave the room and as she did, she glanced over her shoulder. She looked directly at me. She knew Mrs. Patterlin forgot me and she wasn't going to say a word. Her smirk hit me harder than a Yankees' pitch. Somehow I would have to deal with Olivia and her crew, but not now.

Gym was a short walk from Room 25. I remembered that detail from the school tour I got when I registered yesterday. Was it only yesterday?

Chapter 3
Now what?

Sitting in an empty classroom felt weird. With math finished, I pulled out my new purple glitter notebook and started to write.

Journal Entry #1-
Thursday, September 22

Dear Journal,
Well, I've really made a mess of things so far at Foxfield. I'm sure Mrs. Patterlin thinks I'm a trouble-maker and most of the kids probably think I'm weird. Every time I'm the least bit nervous, my right eye starts to vibrate. It drives me crazy. Olivia noticed it and told everyone.

I just lost it and grabbed her ponytail and pulled. Everything got worse after that. Now I'm sitting here alone after being left behind from gym. The "Grade 5 Rules" make me sweat.
I miss my old school. More later.
Gwen

I closed my journal and slid it under my math book. All of a sudden I heard teacher footsteps in the hall; the echo of Mrs. Patterlin's sensible shoes grew louder and louder. I sat up straight, folded my hands on my desk and waited for the worst.

While fingering through her papers with her head tilted down, Mrs. Patterlin entered the room. She sat down at her desk without ever looking up. She jumped slightly in her seat when she noticed me still sitting there.

"Gwendolyn, what are you doing here? Why aren't you at gym?"

My mouth froze at first, but finally my words spilled out like a torn bag of jellybeans.

"I didn't know what to do, Mrs. Patterlin. I was here in time-out and not in my cluster so I waited for you to call me, but you didn't so I knew that I couldn't talk without getting permission first so I raised my hand but you didn't see it so I waved it in the air but I must have been blocked by this bookcase and you didn't see me so I didn't line up and just stayed here. I'm sorry; I just didn't know what to do."

Then my tears flowed as fast as my words and I put my head on my desk.

I felt so stupid. I never cry in school and here I was blubbering like a baby.

"Well, you've had quite a rough day so far, Gwen. Here's a tissue. Now, dry your eyes, get a drink at the bubbler, and get to gym. We'll talk more later."

I headed for the door when I heard her call my name.

"Gwendolyn, would you please come back and push in your chair?"

With my head tipped down and my eyes raised, I dutifully walked back to my chair. This was going to be a long day.

Chapter 4
The Gym Class Disaster

Entering a special class late is not fun.

Walking toward the double doors to the gym, I felt like a mouse about to enter a roomful of hungry cats. Not only was I late, but also I am not what you would call "athletic." I stepped in to find one of my worst gym nightmares – gymnastic equipment! Trampolines, uneven bars, parallel bars and bright blue gym mats sprouted up everywhere on the gym floor. Great. I'm a super mega-klutz at gymnastics! Mr. Santini stood by the parallel bars; I walked slowly toward him and handed him my pass.

"She's the new kid," one of Benny's buddies blurted out from behind the uneven bars.

"Quiet, Joey. I don't remember asking you for your input."

Joey, as I would later learn, always wanted to be first with the news. He'll probably be a news anchorman someday.

Mr. Santini looked like my great uncle Angelo. His almost bald head, wide shoulders and big arms loomed before me. For some reason, that

I'll never know, everyone in my family called my Uncle Angelo "Uncle Chops." Uncle Chops ran a pizza parlor that made the best calzones in Utica, New York. He always acted tough, but he always made me laugh.

"Gwendolyn Claire, is that your name?"

I nodded.

"Ask her about what happened before gym, Mr. S." Benny looked around to make sure everyone was watching him.

The "back cluster boys" guffawed and snickered like they had back in the classroom.

"All right, that's enough. Everyone, up. Heather, over here. The rest of you line up at the outside door. Eight laps around the track. You can thank Benny and Joey for the laps since they chose to break the 'no talking' rule. "

Joey and Benny got their share of pokes and dirty looks as everyone lined up. Olivia, Amanda, and the M&M's slithered over and got into line making sure on their way to throw a few evil eyes in my direction.

"Heather, take Gwen to the girls' locker room so she can change; then meet us on the track. Welcome to Foxfield, Gwen." He quickly shook my hand, patted me on the shoulder and joined the class by the door.

So that was her name, Heather. She was the girl from Cluster #1 who had smiled at me earlier.

"Okay, let's go." The heavy door slammed behind the class and Heather and I stood alone in the empty gym.

"Come on; I'll show you the locker room. I kind of know how you're feeling; I was new to Foxfield four years ago."

"I'll bet you didn't have troubles like I have so far."

"Well, actually . . ." Heather stopped short.

"Go on," I encouraged.

"I'll tell you later. For now just try to forget what happened."

Heather looked like Laura Ingalls from Little House on the Prairie. Swinging back and forth, her long, honey-colored hair swept across the back of her gym suit like a silky waterfall. Her brown eyes smiled even when her mouth didn't.

"Here you go." Heather pointed to a locker. "Just put your stuff in here."

"Thanks, Heather."

"By the way, I don't blame you for grabbing Olivia's ponytail today. I've wanted to a million times.I've been in the same class with her four years in a row."

"You poor thing."

"We used to be friends, believe it or not. I don't know exactly why it happened, but at the beginning of third grade she really turned mean. Now she acts as if she's the queen of England or something. At any rate, let's just say that she's not a very nice person. Something else you should know – she's sort of the teacher's pet."

"Great. Whose hair do I almost pull out of her head? Olivia's, the teacher's pet."

"Relax, Gwen. Let's get outside. I'm glad we're running track. I always dread gymnastics; I feel like such a klutz."

"Me too," I seconded.

Heather and I sprinted toward the door and pushed out into the warm September sun. Meeting a new friend is always a plus, especially on a day like today.

Chapter 5
Disaster Relief

Heather helped me to the nurse's office. Yes, the nurse's office. While following Hermy, the chubby, curly, red-haired kid in cluster #4 too closely down the final turn on the track, I collided with him when he bent over to catch his breath. I jammed my foot into the back of his foot, flew over the top of him, and landed on my knees on the gritty track. I felt my little right toe bend in a weird direction. My scrapped knees immediately started bleeding and dripped down the front of my legs. Great, Gwen, why not bring even more attention to yourself? Heather, running next to me, called out to Mr. Santini who sent us to see Mrs. Muller, the school nurse.

Mrs. Muller, with medium length dark brown hair, a long slim frame, and standing even taller than "Hawkeye" Patterlin, stood talking on the phone at her desk. She signaled us in with her long pointer finger and directed us to the cots. Heather grabbed some paper towels on the way to put on my knees. I removed my right sneaker to see how my little toe was doing.

Looking kind of purple and blue, the toe throbbed with pain and I knew that I would be hobbling for at least a couple of days.

"Yes, Mrs. Newman; that would be fine." She balanced the phone while she reached for band-aids and first aid spray. "My office is open until 4:00; I'll see you then." Hanging up the phone, Mrs. Muller spoke in a voice that rang like a bell.

"Hi, Heather and friend. What have we here? Did you crash land on a strange planet?"

How did she know that was exactly how I felt?

"Hi, Mrs. Muller," Heather laughed. "This is Gwen. Hermy stopped to catch his breath on the track during gym class just now and Gwen tripped over him."

"Tripped over Hermy? Boy, that's quite a feat," Mrs. Muller said smiling while she took a long hard look at my toe and cleaned my knees and legs. "Gwen, if I clean you up and put a couple of handy-dandy all purpose band-aids on your knees and a tight bandage around your badly-bruised-but-not-broken toe, do you think you can make it through the day or should I call your mom and have her pick you up?"

"No, don't call Mom. I'm fine, really." I certainly didn't want to bother Mom at her new job.

"Okay, then. I think you'll be fine too." Mrs. Muller stood up and helped me to my feet as she walked toward the refrigerator. "Heather, please help Gwen back to the classroom. Gwen, if your toe or your knees bother you later this afternoon, just let Mrs. Patterlin know and I'll see what I can do to help. Slide your foot back into your sneaker and lace it up loosely. Here's a cold pack in case you need it."

"Thanks, Mrs. Muller," Heather and I said at the same time. We looked at each other, laughed, hooked little fingers, and each made a wish.

"You've picked a great new friend for yourself, Gwen," Mrs. Muller added with a smile.

I leaned on Heather's arm for support and looked at her smiling face.

I knew Mrs. Muller was right.

Chapter 6
Language Arts

Crunching on the peppermints Mrs. Muller had given us, Heather and I hurried back to our language arts lesson. As we approached the room, we held our breaths, shared a courageous look and bee-lined to our seats. Seated in cluster #1 near the door, Heather didn't have far to walk. My time-out desk by the window required me to pass in front of everyone including Mrs. Patterlin who stood at the overhead.

"So how are you, Gwendolyn? Will you survive?"

"Yes, Mrs. Patterlin," I said, wishing she had just ignored me. I could almost feel Olivia's nasty smirk piercing my brain as I hurried to my seat.

"Good. Now class, so Heather and Gwendolyn understand the assignment, I will repeat the procedure."

Benny, Joey and the rest of the "back cluster boys" groaned in unison.

"That's enough, boys. It won't hurt any of you to hear the assignment again. In fact, Benny, would *you* like to tell the girls about the lesson?"

"That's all right, Mrs. Patterlin. You can do it much better than I can."

"Thank you for the encouragement, Benny."Mrs. Patterlin did not look pleased at all.

"Now, class, the first and most important part of your assignment is to use your imagination."

I liked the assignment already. We could actually *use* our imaginations. So much of our writing, since third grade at least, had been to prepare for the dreaded "State Tests."

"Hawkeye" continued.

"Line leaders, could you please help me distribute these papers? And let's not forget Gwen by the window." Mrs. Patterlin smiled a friendly smile in my direction.

The title of the assignment was "My Own Island." What a cool topic. First we had to fill out some lists: 5 people your age that you would bring and why, 6 foods/drinks and why, 12 articles of clothing/shoes and why, 3 medicines and why, 3 books and why, and 3 "anything else" and why. Water, shelter, furniture, blankets, towels, soap and dental supplies would be provided. It seemed easy at first, but filling in the lists wasn't easy. This would take some thought.

In what seemed like only five minutes, I felt a tap on my shoulder and looked up to see Mrs. Patterlin.

"Gwen, are you ready for lunch?"

I looked at the clock and then at the door to see all my classmates already lined up. Time always passed so quickly when I was really *into* something. Heather caught my eye from the end of the girls' line and waved me over.

"You were so engrossed in your work that you didn't even hear me call lunchtime; I'm impressed." Mrs. Patterlin smiled at me with her full-toothed smile. "You must really enjoy writing."

Mrs. Patterlin was right; I did love writing.I've written stories in my notebooks at home since I was little. Before I learned how to read or write, I told Mom my stories and she wrote them down for me. I even turned my dreams into stories.

"By the way, Gwen, when we get back from lunch you may go back to your cluster."

"Thanks, Mrs. Patterlin." I jumped up, pushed in my chair, and slid in behind Heather in line.

"Zip and flip. Ivan. Vlad. Are you ready or do we all have to sit down and start over again?"

Ivan and Vlad never lost a chance to speak to each other in Russian even if it meant getting into trouble in the lunch line. They nodded their heads in unison and we left for the cafeteria. I have to admit, they were kind of funny.

Chapter 7
Lunch

Heather and I, our trays filled with the pizza special, headed for our class's tables near the stage. Foxfield had a combination cafeteria/ auditorium. Andrew and Hermy sat alone at the end of the table closest to the door. Andrew's nose practically touched the mystery book that he had been reading in between work all morning. Glued to his hand like another part of his body, the book followed him everywhere he went. I also realized that the only time I had heard Andrew's voice was when he had been annoyed with Olivia.

I leaned my head toward Heather. "Does he ever speak?"

"Who?"

"Andrew."

Just as we slid into our spots, Heather whispered, "Watch this."

"Hey, Andrew, what's the latest on <u>The Mystery of the Severed Hand</u>?"

"You won't believe it. Remember the secret staircase that Mason found after his magic pencil rolled behind the bookcase?"

"Sure, I remember. The pencil bumped the wall and a panel slid back."

Andrew nodded his head excitedly.

"Well, it turns out that it leads to his grandmother's kitchen and actually takes him back in time to when his mother was a little girl."

"Cool. What happens next?" I chimed in.

"Well, actually, I haven't gotten much further than his finding out that it actually *is* his grandmother's kitchen, but I'll let you know when I do." Andrew's glasses slipped down his nose and he hurried to straighten them. He looked over at me. "Gwen, right?"

"Yes, that's me. I thought I would have become world famous by now."

"I wasn't sure about your name because when I'm reading I kind of block out everything else. Sorry."

"That's fine with me. I wish everyone would block out this morning."

"Listen, Gwen; Olivia needed to be taught a lesson. She gets on my nerves, too.Remember: her desk is right in front of mine."

Hermy looked up from his third piece of pizza, nodded, and spoke with his mouth still half full. "Yeah, she's a royal pain in the neck. She's always in *my* face. Hey, Gwen, I'm sorry I tripped you in gym. I'm not the best runner and I'm always in the way. How are your knees?"

"Fine. Just fine. I should have been looking where I was going."

The pizza wasn't half bad and lunch sped by. The four of us kept talking until we were called to line up at the door. Olivia's table stood to line up first and as she passed by, she shoved me. She timed it so that neither Mrs. Lucente nor Mrs. Foster, the teacher aides, saw her.When I turned quickly to see who had pushed me, I caught the bottom of my shirt on the rough table edge and tore a hole in it. Great. Let's add a torn shirt to my list of first day blunders.

Heather looked at the tear. "Don't worry about it, Gwen; it looks like something that your mom can fix in a minute. As for "Witchie-Poo" let's pretend that nothing happened. She'll hate that more than anything."

"You're right, Heather; she's not worth it."

So with new courage, we zipped, flipped and headed for Room 25.

Chapter 8
Recess

The walk down the hall was uneventful; that is, until we rounded the corner and headed for bathroom break. Standing by the drinking fountain were Olivia, Amanda, and the M&M's. Now what? Olivia stepped forward and shoved my shoulder with her pointer finger.

"Hey, Claire, do you think you're going to get away with what happened this morning so easy? Nobody tries to make an idiot out of me and gets away with it."

After I regained my balance, I froze. With minds of their own, my lips locked, my right eye started twitching and my stomach began a roller coaster ride.

Heather spoke up.

"Leave her alone, Olivia. Gwen wasn't the one trying to make trouble. If you hadn't picked on her, none of this would have happened. Consider it over."

"Why don't you mind your own business, Sebastian; this has nothing to do with you."

"Yes, it does. Gwen just happens to be my friend."

I slowly glanced over at Heather who suddenly looked different. Her gentle face had turned to stone and her brown eyes, usually filled with a smile, punctured the air and drilled into Olivia's space.

"Friend, is it? Whose side are you on anyway, Heather? Claire's new here; she's not a Foxfield girl like you and me. She doesn't belong." Amanda and the M&M's nodded to each other.

"If bullying someone is part of being a Foxfield girl, count me out."

"Oh, I did, Heather, a long time ago," Olivia whipped back, "but we (the girls and I) thought we might give you another chance to rejoin the Foxfield Four and make it the Foxfield Five again."

Just as Heather opened her mouth to speak, Mrs. Mendez (another fifth grade teacher) and Mrs. Patterlin stepped into the hall; we must have been getting loud. "Hawkeye" called to us.

"Girls, what's going on down there? Get your drinks and get back here immediately."

Olivia smiled with faked sweetness in Mrs. Patterlin's direction and answered in a syrupy voice. "Sorry, Mrs. Patterlin. Coming, Mrs. Patterlin." Then under her breath she muttered to us "We'll continue this later." Olivia and her fan club turned to go.

Just then a voice boomed over the loud speaker. "Attention fifth grade teachers: due to wet, rainy conditions on the playground, recess will be held in the library today. To repeat: fifth grade recess will take place in the library today. "

I still hadn't used the restroom and now I really needed to go.

"Go ahead, Heather; I'll be right there."

At least we wouldn't have to face Olivia and the rest on the playground. The library felt much safer. Library recess meant we would be watching a DVD or hearing a story; the playground sometimes turned into a free-for-all, especially when the playground monitors weren't looking.

"I'll wait," Heather called over her shoulder as she stared the others down the hall.

I used the girls' room as quickly as I could and joined Heather in the hall.

"Let's sit far away from them in the library."

"My thoughts completely," Heather added.

Trying to join our class without being seen was impossible. As we moved toward the library, Mrs. Patterlin gave us one of her "I'm not pleased" looks and Olivia threw us one of her glares. My eye still twitched and my stomach still rumbled.

Although recess included a video that I had seen about ten times, the Foxfield Four sat on the opposite side of the library and I was happy for the peace and quiet of the dark room and the familiar story.

Chapter 9
Cursive

"Okay, class, take out your cursive workbooks and turn to page 10. We're working on our m's today."

Cursive writing. Yikes. I'm a lefty and cursive is really hard for me. Olivia carefully placed her notebook and poised herself for her right-handed writing. Great. My left-handed elbow lined up directly with Olivia's right-handed elbow. Sitting up with perfect posture, she directed her usual smile at Mrs. Patterlin who stood at the overhead. (If you look up "brown-noser" in the dictionary, I'm sure you'll see a picture of "Livi Dear".) Of all the desks in the classroom, why did mine have to be next to hers?

"Okay, everyone. Remember: sit with both feet flat on the floor, tip your paper, and place your non-writing hand on the top corner of your paper so the paper stays still. Is everyone ready?"

Olivia's right hand flew up and almost hit me in the face.

"Yes, Livi?"

"Gwen's elbow is in my way." Olivia whined in her whiniest voice. "How can I possibly do my best cursive if <u>she's</u> in my way?" Olivia aimed the word "she's" in my direction.

Her voice gnawed at me like a dentist's drill. I tried not to roll my eyes.

Without even checking where my elbow was, Mrs. Patterlin turned to me. "Miss Claire, please assist your classmate by moving a bit to your right."

"Of course, Mrs. Patterlin."

I moved my chair two inches to the right. When Mrs. Patterlin's eyes were back on the overhead, (you guessed it) Olivia also shifted her seat two inches to the right. Now what? Again her right hand flew up into the air.

"Mrs. Patterlin, Mrs. Patterlin, I still don't have room. It's not fair. Gwen is trying to ruin my cursive on purpose. She hates me; I just know it."

Then the drama continued. Tears. OMG. Tears flowed down her face like she had lost her newest "Glitter Gloss." A virtual Mount Vesuvious of tears. What a drama queen.

"I'm going to tell my mother what happened today." Olivia squealed like a piglet with her head stuck between fence posts. "I've just had an awful day."

During lunch Heather had warned me about Olivia's mother. Mrs. Roberts, the president of the Parent/Teacher Group at Foxfield, influenced just about everything that went on at Foxfield. None of the teachers, including Mrs. Patterlin, wanted to make the P.T.G. president angry.

On Grammie's bookshelf is <u>How to Make Friends and Influence People</u>; I think it's a book I desperately need to read.

"Okay, ladies, I have a quick solution to your problem. Move your desks to each other's spot. That way Gwen's elbow will be on the outside and so will yours, Livi dear. Nobody's elbow will be bumped."

An easy solution. Thank goodness. "Livi Dear" and I slid our desks around each other. Now I was directly opposite Andrew's desk; he smiled, leaned forward, and pointed to Olivia behind his hand. "At least now I won't have to look straight into that face every minute of the day."

The lesson continued and Olivia focused on her cursive instead of on me.

Chapter 10
"End of the Day" Work Time

Mrs. Patterlin gave us the last part of the day to finish our assignments or to continue our "island" writing. With all my other work done, I needed an escape so I pulled out my language arts notebook to see where I had left off. After glancing over my lists, I realized that I needed to change some stuff and to finish the first list. It's funny. Earlier in the day I couldn't complete the "people" list, but now I could: Heather, Andrew, and Hermy. Maybe today hadn't been so bad after all.

Okay, now for an escape to my island. I just let my imagination fly.

When the helicopter flew me over the island, I couldn't see much at first because of the grey fog that covered everything like my favorite sweatshirt. Then after circling for a few minutes, a clear patch opened up to reveal a waterfall. I laughed with excitement as the hole got bigger and bigger and an incredible sight met my eyes. The whole island looked just like my favorite amusement park in Canobie

Lake, New Hampshire. The huge sky ride circled and circled like the giant wheel of a bicycle. I felt as if I could touch it if I just reached out the door of the copter. The waterfall turned out to be the incredible flume ride that splashed and covered the whole walkway nearby. Ride after ride stretched to cover the whole landscape. Booths and shops with everything from cotton candy, to t-shirts, to Italian ice filled in the spaces. Around every shop and ride, gardens and gardens of sunflowers, petunias, and roses looked like jewels placed in a lovely broach. As the helicopter approached the landing pad, I noticed a lovely white cottage in the middle of one of the gardens.

"That's where you'll be staying. There's a schedule inside of when the others will be arriving. Also inside you'll find everything else you'll need; plus all the other items promised you when you won the contest." The pilot, who looked an awful lot like my grandpa, finished his explanation and then smoothly landed the copter. After helping me out and handing me my carry on bag, he wished me good luck and flew off. I was all alone on my island or was I?

Chapter 11
Free Time

"Hey, Gwen, it's 3:00 o'clock; we can stop work now. How about some puzzles until dismissal?"

Heather had slid into Olivia's chair while Witchie-Poo, somewhere else in the room, took advantage of "free time" to gossip.

"Sure, Heather," I answered, sounding very much as if I had just awakened from a dream.

"I could hardly get your attention."

"Heather, it may sound geeky, but I think this island project is really cool."

"Yeah, it is pretty cool. I'm still working on my lists, but I'm almost done with them. You're on my 'People List' of course."

"You're on mine too. Let's not tell each other what we write; that way when we share the stories they'll be a total surprise."

"Sounds like a plan. Now, how about those puzzles? Mrs. Patterlin has these neat block puzzles that are plastic cubes chopped into pieces; you have to put the pieces together into a complete perfect cube. Believe me, it sounds easy but it's not. There are five and I've only solved the blue one since school started. Jacob's already solved four of them."

"I bet I can solve one before school's over today," I challenged. "Let's go!"

Chapter 12
Dismissal

"Attention, everyone. Please put all puzzles, games and books in their proper spots; then take your seats and put your 'Go Home Folder' on your desk. Don't forget that there's a spelling test tomorrow. Also remember to continue work on your language arts project. Jared and Livi, please pass out the daily notes. Remember, boys and girls, I expect all notes to be signed by your parents and returned tomorrow."

The daily note. I had forgotten all about that. I hated disappointing Mom. Jared and Olivia swooped around the room like vultures ready to devour their prey. My 4th grade teacher used daily notes too so they were nothing new to me. I prayed that Jared had my note. He was passing them out as quickly as he could. He wasn't *reading* them. Olivia, on the other hand, read each and every one. Looking angry, she approached me but stopped short to whisper to Amanda on the way. They both glared at me before Olivia threw my note toward my desk. It fell at my feet. I leaned to pick it up and bumped my head on the corner of the desk.

"Are you all right?" Amanda snickered sarcastically. Amanda had joined Olivia while she gave out the daily notes.

Olivia added her fake apology. "Sorry, Gwen, it slipped out of my hand."

As the two of them moved around the room, they looked back over their shoulders at me and continued with their gossipy whispers.

I remembered what Heather had said earlier in the day about ignoring them so I turned away and pretended to be busy with the inside of my desk. Andrew, stuffing his homework in his folder, leaned forward.

"Olivia and Amanda make the Wicked Witch of the West and her sister look good."

Andrew made me laugh in spite of the sore spots on the top of my head and in my heart. I had totally forgotten about my knees and toe. I smiled, closed my eyes, grimaced and turned over my note. Gradually I opened my eyes and the words came into focus.

"Dear Mrs. Claire, although Gwendolyn had a difficult morning, the remainder of her day went well. I'm sure she will fill you in on the details. I am confident that Gwendolyn will soon feel comfortable at Foxfield Elementary. Sincerely, Mrs. Patterlin."

I could breathe again. "Hawkeye" Patterlin had given me a second chance. Now I knew why Olivia and Amanda were so upset.

Chapter 13
Going Home

"First dismissal students, please push in your chairs and line up at the door. That's you, Gwen. 'First dismissal' means that you are being picked up by your parents."

As I walked down the hall, I could see Mom standing in the lobby. Even taller than Mrs. Patterlin, my mother can best be described in one word "beautiful;" I may be prejudiced, but even my friends tell me how pretty she is. Her green eyes and chestnut hair look great together. Mom is definitely cool too. She's the perfect mix of mother and best friend. She expects me to do my best and her rules stand strong, but I can always talk to her about anything. She told me once that the little kid in her was "still alive and well." I think I know what she means. She hasn't forgotten how hard it is sometimes to be a kid. My father left us a month before I was born so it's been just the two of us for ten years already. We count on each other no matter what.

Mom's hug felt great after this long and complicated day.

"So how was your day?"

I hesitated.

"Interesting" was the only word I could think of and it kind of fit the day.

"Interesting, huh?"

"I'll tell you more when we get home. Okay, Mom?"

"Sure. Hey, why are you hobbling?"

"It's no big deal, but it is part of why today was interesting."

"I can't wait to hear the details." Mom smiled as she put her arm around my shoulder.

Upon pushing open the exit door, we ran through the downpour to our car. The afternoon had flown by so quickly that I hadn't even noticed that it was still raining.

I enjoyed the quiet on the way home as my "daily note," just waiting to be delivered, lay in my backpack.

Chapter 14
"Down Time"

After work and school, Mom and I need what we call our "down time." She pulls out the newspaper, brews a small pot of tea and heads for her favorite chair in the living room. I grab a glass of chocolate milk and a few vanilla wafers and go upstairs to my room to start homework.

"Supper at 6, Gwen." Mom kisses me on the cheek. "We'll talk about your 'interesting' day then. No worries, Honey." I think Mom can read my mind and my heart.

"Thanks, Mom."

I felt better already. I scurried upstairs to my room, shoved open the door with my "bum," dropped my backpack on the floor, and carefully placed my snack on my desk.

I just loved our new townhouse, especially my room. The bay window behind my window seat overlooked the shared backyard of our townhouse complex. Pink cushions filled the area and the sun streamed in every afternoon at this time. I could stretch out completely to read or write in my journal. Aside from my bed, it was my favorite spot. Just before my eighth birthday, I had begged for a canopy bed. Well, Mom gave in "this time" and on my birthday a new bed with a blue cloud canopy arrived. I imagined it to be my personal magic carpet.

I wolfed down my snack, pulled my pink glitter notebook out of my backpack, grabbed my favorite blue gel pen, and flopped onto the window seat. I couldn't wait to get back to my island. It was already starting to feel real, as if I could actually go there whenever I wanted to. I could. I could go there whenever I wanted to, like right now.

I turned slowly around; straight ahead stood my dream cottage.

Standing two stories tall with a wrap-around porch, my pure white cottage sparkled in the sunshine. Pink shutters cupped each window in their protective hands. Lacey curtains peeked out and promised me that the inside of my new island home would be just as wonderful. An English garden like the ones in my mother's garden magazines decorated the slate pathway to my front door. Heliotrope, daisies, roses of all imaginable colors and long, wavy grasses danced in the island wind. Moving slowly like in a dream, I walked toward the door. Without my even touching it, the chiffon pink door gradually opened.

"Gwen, are you ready for dinner?" Mom's voice echoed up the stairs; slightly startled, I dropped my pen and suddenly I was back in my room. The island felt so fresh in my brain, like the feeling you have when you first wake up from a beautiful dream that you don't want to end. Wanting to step into my cottage, I called back to her.

"Mom, can we eat a little later?"

"It's 6 already; I thought that you might be hungry by now."

I couldn't believe it. I had been in my room for two hours. It had felt like two minutes.

"Okay, Mom, I'll be down in a minute."

I closed my notebook, placed it carefully on the cushioned seat, and watched as the early evening sun set the cover sparkling. How I loved to write. I hurried down the stairs but stopped halfway down when I remembered my daily note. I had forgotten all about it while I was on my island. "On my island." Those words were becoming so real to me. For two whole hours I had escaped into a dream. Digging in my backpack, I wondered how I would tell Mom about the day's events. Clutching the note in my hand, I headed down the stairs.

Chapter 15
The Daily Note Revealed

The wonderful smell of spaghetti and meatballs, my grandmother's recipe, made my mouth water as I slipped my daily note next to Mom's napkin. Usually I set the table, but today Mom had beaten me to it. Ripping salad greens into a bowl on the kitchen counter, she spoke to me over her shoulder.

"Did you take a nap up there? You were so quiet; I thought you might have dozed off."

"No, at least I don't think I did."

"Do you have a lot of homework?"

Mom, in her own sweet way, started to ask about my first day at Foxfield. The time had come. She brought the salad to the table and we sat down. I loved this little dining area. It was right near the sliding doors that led to the deck that overlooked the garden. Leafy trees and fresh flowers still filled the September scenery.

"No, not much." I answered Mom with the fewest words I could while concentrating on twisting the spaghetti on my fork. "I have a spelling test tomorrow and I have to continue working on my language arts project."

I could feel Mom's eyes on me as I continued to twist my spaghetti.

"Well, that's good."

A long pause filled the space usually filled with conversation. Mom and I don't ever sit so quietly unless there's really something on one of our minds.

"Is something wrong, Honey? You're doing a great job twisting your spaghetti, but I don't think that any has reached your mouth yet."

Mom had been so focused on me that she hadn't noticed the note near her napkin. She picked up her napkin without looking and I watched as my daily note fell to the floor.

This was my chance to put off the whole thing until later.

Instead I got up from my seat, went around to her side of the table and stooped to pick up the note. Standing there like a marble statue, I handed Mom the note.

"What's this?"

"My daily note."

"Oh, let's see how you did today." As I rounded the table to go back to my chair, Mom unfolded the now wrinkled paper, smoothed it out and began to read. She didn't say a word until she finished, folded it back in half, and laid it on the table between us.

"Tough day, huh, Gwen?" Her sympathetic voice soothed me.

"That's for sure." My head couldn't have hung any lower without touching the table.

"So Mrs. Patterlin said you would fill me in on the details." Mom's voice remained firm but warm.

"Yes." I could barely get the word out of my mouth. My tightening throat squeezed tears into the corners of my eyes.

I slowly began filling her in on every miserable moment; as a kind of cushion, I added the good parts too. She listened, as she always does, very quietly, and didn't say a thing until my words ran out. My spaghetti had gotten cold and so had my hands. Finally I gathered some courage and looked up into her smiling face.

"Sweetie, my day wasn't that great either. Starting a new job is like starting a new school. You don't know anyone. You have to figure out what's expected of you. Everything is new and different. Most people are kind, but some are not. Unfortunately, you have to work with the not-so-nice people too. All of us get frustrated now and then, especially when someone hurts our feelings for no reason. The trick is to keep yourself from striking back while protecting those feelings and that's not easy, especially when you're only 10 years old. Here I am 33 and I still have to hold myself back sometimes."

"Really, Mom?"

"Really, Honey."

"Now, I am not saying that what you did was in any way okay. Do you understand?"

"Yes, I understand."

"Tomorrow's another day and you'll have to figure out how to get along with Olivia and the rest. It does sound though that you've made some good friends too."

"Oh, I have, Mom. I really have."

"That's what I want to hear. Do you think that you can make tomorrow a better day?"

"I'm going to try; that's for sure."

"Good. Now get me a pen so I can write Mrs. Patterlin a short note."

I handed her a pen and waited while she finished writing.

"Put this in your backpack so you'll be all set for tomorrow. I'll warm up your spaghetti."

I rushed upstairs, tucked the note away, and hurried downstairs to finish supper.

After devouring two bowls of blueberry fizz jello with whipped cream and two cherries, I cleaned off the table and filled up the dishwasher while Mom asked me my spelling words. I found spelling to be easy and I always felt sorry for my friends who dreaded spelling tests each week.

"Good job." Mom handed me my list. "What are you going to do until bedtime?"

"Could I sit out in the garden for awhile and write? I know it'll be dark in about half an hour, but I promise to come inside in about twenty minutes."

"Sure, why not. Just make sure to stay right outside the sliding doors."

"Thanks, Mom." I hurried to my room, grabbed my notebook off the window seat, flew down the stairs, slid open the doors, and entered the garden.

Chapter 16
Back to My Island

I love September because it's still a little summery but the air is putting on its fall coolness too. My favorite warm fuzzy sweatshirt hugged me. I opened my notebook and with hardly a thought began to write.

Without my even touching it, the chiffon pink door gradually opened to reveal a huge living area with large soft pink and white striped couches with lime pillows. Each couch faced the center of the room where a huge round table topped with pink, white and lime mosaic tiles stood. I slipped off my shoes and stood still while I let my eyes discover what they could. Just beyond the living room lay a shiny welcoming kitchen. A glittering spiral staircase, its steps covered in plush pink carpeting, wound up to a landing that encircled the outside of the whole first floor. Off the landing were the bedrooms; the door to each room was labeled in gold letters with the names of the people on my list: Heather and I in the first, Andrew and Hermy in the second, and Olivia and Amanda in the third. (Hey, every story needs a bad guy or two.) Standing before the door, I touched each letter with the tips of my fingers and then reached for the doorknob.I had always wanted a sister and sharing the room with Heather would be almost like having a sister for real.

"Gwen. Time to come in. It's bedtime."

Mom's voice seemed to come from far away.

"Coming, Mom."

The sun's rays just barely peeked above the horizon. Clutching my notebook to my chest, I hurried into the house with a light heart.

Chapter 17
Before Bed

While brushing my teeth, I stared at myself in the mirror and started to laugh through my foaming peppermint teeth. I looked like a jungle beast with rabies. After spitting and rinsing, I reached for my face cleanser, soaped up and splashed off the suds.

Mom and I have a kind of ritual every night before I go to bed. After my bathroom routine, I meet her in the old, cushy recliner in our living room. It's getting harder and harder for the two of us to fit in the chair together, but we still manage with a little effort. Then comes what we call the "How was our day?" conversation. That's when we talk about the good things about our day. What did we learn, enjoy, realize, etc. The lists vary in length from day to day, but the main thing is to really think hard about the day.

"So how was your day, Gwen?"

"Well, I guess I'd give it an overall rating of four stars out of five."

"Hey, that's pretty good."

"Yeah, especially since my morning was a one at best."

"So what finally made it a four star day?"

"Four great things."

"Oh, really. What?"

"Well, the first thing is making a good friend named Heather."

"Making a good friend is always worthy of a star."

"The second star is for getting a teacher who asks me to use my imagination and is willing to give me a second chance."

"Definitely worth a star."

"My third star goes to you, Mom, for being an understanding mother."

"I do have my not- so-understanding days once in while."

"Well, today you were perfect."

"Thanks, Honey. What's the 4th star for?"

"My island."

"Your island?"

"It started out as my language arts project, Mom, but it's more than that now."

"It sounds as if you're having fun with your writing again, Honey. When can I read it?"

"Well, I've only started it, but . . . how about right now?"

"Great."

I jumped off the chair and hurried upstairs for my notebook. Usually we read a favorite book before bed, but tonight we were reading something by a new author. Me.

Time flew by until Mom tucked me in for the night. She actually loved my story so far and that made me feel super. September's chilly nights made for great sleeping.As I pulled my poufy down comforter up to my chin, I closed my eyes and imagined my island bedroom behind its gold-lettered door. My imagination played with the possibilities for my room as I slowly drifted off to sleep.

Chapter 18
Friday before School

I woke up before the alarm today with my island bedroom fresh in my mind. My dreams had taken me through the door. As I pulled aside the curtains, the sun lit up the sparkles on my pink notebook. I flipped it open, slid out my pen and spilled my words onto the paper.

Just then I heard the sound of the door sliding open downstairs.

"Hello? Anybody here?"

It was Heather.

"I'm up here." I peeked over the balcony to see Heather dropping her purple backpack on the floor.

"Hi. Thank goodness you're here."

"Where else would I be? Didn't my map help?"

"I looked on the ice cream stand counter where you said you would leave the map to your cottage, but the map was missing. So I made a mental map from what

I remembered from seeing your cottage from the air. I must have made some wrong turns, and finally, after two hours of walking, I saw your cottage in the distance. I must admit that I was starting to panic. Not only was the map missing, but I had this weird feeling that I was being watched."

By this time Heather had reached the landing.

"Anything is possible; although I don't think that anyone else is here yet. The whole thing is kind of freaky. We'll check into it later; I promise. Right now I'm just glad you're here."

"Me too."

"I was just about to enter our room when you came in. Look." I pointed to our names on the door. "Ready?"

Heather nodded. I turned the gold knob and pushed the door over the thick pink and purple carpet.

Frozen in our spots with our mouths hanging open, we gazed around a dream room. Each of us had a canopy bed. Heather's purple and white canopy bed and my pink and white canopy bed lined up against the wall opposite the door. Flowing, silky sheer curtains, caressed by the island breeze from the opened window, enclosed each bed. Our names, again in gold, hung above each headboard. In front of the huge bay window on the far left wall, a thick velvet cushion in a purple and pink checkerboard print covered the window seat from wall to wall. At each end big, velvety matching cushions lay propped against the wall. Vanities in pink for me and purple for Heather hugged the wall to the left of the door. The cushions on each stool matched the other pillows in the room. Pictures of our favorite people from family to rock stars to sports figures covered the walls. Our bare feet sank into the cushy carpet as we danced around the room.

"Whee! Do you even believe it?" Heather screamed, while spinning in a circle. She hopped up to the window seat, jumped off and plopped on her bed.

I did the same.

Looking up we discovered a huge skylight that revealed a cloudless blue sky.

"It's just like I said I wanted it to be." I gasped out of breath.

"You've got a great imagination. It's just perfect. Thanks for putting me on your list."

"My pleasure."

I couldn't believe how soft my bed was. I felt as if I were sinking into a cloud. Perhaps I would just lie here for a minute or two. Heather seemed to agree since she stopped her usual chatter. About five minutes later a bell sounded in the hall. Heather popped up and slowly opened the door.

"Gwen. Honey, it's late. Dress quickly. My alarm didn't go off." Mom's voice sounded panicky.

"Coming." I slammed shut my notebook, flew into my bathroom to brush my teeth and splash water on my face; threw on my pink shirt, my favorite jeans, pink socks and sneakers; slid my notebook and homework into my backpack; and headed for the stairs. Mom waited by the door with a granola bar, a yogurt and a juice box in her hand.

"Our lunches and jackets are already in the car, kiddo; let's fly."

I hurried to the car while Mom locked the door. Before I knew it, Foxfield School stood before me like a castle and I, the first-ever pre-teen female knight in shining armor, felt ready to face any dragons that might lurk behind its gates. My imagination was already running wild today; my clearing the air with Mom last night, the good night's sleep, and my early morning writing made me feel like another adventure waited just around the corner.

Chapter 19
The Disappearance

The aisle between the cubby rack and the clusters was pretty tight because lots of the kids didn't push in their backpacks far enough. Hermy's cubby reminded me of Hermy. His jacket stuck out into the aisle and though his gym sneakers were tied together, one lay in the bottom of the cubby and the other hung out on to the floor. His over-flowing folders and books, piled this way and that, filled the top. Hermy shoved over to let me through.

"Hi, Gwen." Hermy's smile looked like a picket fence.

"Hi, Hermy."

"How are your knees?"

"Don't even think about it; I'm fine."

I headed for my desk.

"Hey, Gwen, don't forget to bring your snack to your desk too."

"I forgot to bring one. I guess I'll survive until lunch."

"Here."

Hermy handed me a small bag of Fruit Chewies.

"My mom always packs me two of everything. Two snacks, two sandwiches, two drinks; you get the idea. I guess that *I'll* survive until lunch." Hermy patted his round belly.

"Thanks, Hermy. Are you sure?"

"Don't even think about it; I'm fine."

Hermy was definitely cool.

I made a diagonal across the room toward my desk. As I glanced toward Cluster 1, I noticed that Heather hadn't shown up yet.

Dead ahead the Foxfield Four hovered like a swarm of hornets.

"Excuse me."

"Why? Did you fart or something?" Olivia sneered.

Giggling together, the Foxfield Four looked at me as if I were a moldy, tuna fish sandwich.

I counted to ten in my brain.

"Well? Did you?" Amanda added.

Just then Mrs. Patterlin clapped her hands three times. Even a newcomer like me knew that any Foxfield teacher's three claps meant to stop talking and pay attention.

"Ladies and gentlemen, in your seats by the time I count to five. One, two . . ."

Olivia and her crew stepped aside and I quickly slid through and over to my seat. Today definitely wouldn't be easy. Mrs. Patterlin took attendance.

"All here. Very good."

I raised my hand.

"Yes, Miss Claire?"

"Excuse me, Mrs. Patterlin, but Heather isn't here."

"Heather's at the Lost and Found, Gwendolyn. She seems to have misplaced her language arts notebook. By the way, if any of you finds Heather's notebook, please return it to her immediately."

Just then I saw the M&M's, Molly and Maggie of the Foxfield Four, leaning in to each other and giggling as they looked over at Olivia and

Amanda. Olivia put her finger up to her lips and gave them a dirty look. That was definitely weird.

"Now, everyone, make sure you have put your names on your daily notes and placed them in the basket on my desk. I will collect yesterday's signed note while you begin your morning task. It's a challenging division paper; so be careful. Be sure to check your work."

Just then Heather entered the room and crossed over to Mrs. Patterlin's desk with her pass.

"No luck, Miss Heather?" Mrs. Patterlin asked.

Heather shook her head.

"Don't worry about it now. It'll show up."

"But I wrote for about two hours on my island project last night."

"Do you remember where you left off?"

"Yes."

"Then here's what you'll do. During Language Arts, begin where you left off on some loose-leaf paper. If you brought your notebook to school, I'm sure someone will find it and turn it in before the end of the day. Did you have your name and our room number on it?"

"Yes, but . . . ."

"No more about it now, dear. Go back to your seat and start your day."

Heather passed by me on the way back to her seat and gave me an "I'll tell you about it later" look. Something rotten was going on and I guessed that the Foxfield Four had something to do with it.

Chapter 20
Major Distraction

Journal Entry:
Friday, September 23

Dear Journal,
I don't have any definite proof yet, but I think the Foxfield Four took Heather's notebook to get back at her. Heather looks really sad. I can't help but think that she would have a much easier time of it if I hadn't come to Foxfield. I'll find out more during Art. More later.
Gwen

I closed my journal. Math was already done. Now what? Okay, one more time – it never hurts to look over spelling words one more time:

winning, entering, their, there, they're, computer, minor, language, hinder, and **wondered.** With a few minutes to spare before Art, I decided to practice the words by writing silly sentences.

1. After <u>winning</u> the race, Olivia ran to the judge and grabbed the blue ribbon from his hand.
2. Upon <u>entering</u> the stage, Gwen, not the most graceful dancer in the universe, slipped, fell and landed in the orchestra pit.
3. <u>Their</u> instruments lay <u>there</u> on the floor while the musicians lifted Gwen back on to the stage; <u>they're</u> probably still laughing about it today.
4. Andrew's <u>computer</u> . . . .

Three claps echoed throughout the room.

"Attention, everyone. It's time for Art. Today's line leaders, Maggie and Andrew, please line up at the door."

As we lined up for Art, Heather caught my attention.

"Sit with me," she mouthed.

Chapter 21
Art-ful Dodging

Left of the exit to the playground sat the art room. Mrs. Baxter, a petite lady not much taller than a tall sixth grader, greeted us with a smile. According to Payal, the sixth grader who had given me the Foxfield tour, Mrs. Baxter not only taught Art, but actually was a talented artist too; Foxfield Fine Arts Museum displayed her portraits of children and horses annually. Our school was lucky to have her.

Usually teachers made you sit in a certain seat, but not Mrs. Baxter. Heather and I headed for the small table near the window. Luckily, the table only held four people and Andrew and Hermy took the remaining two seats. The Foxfield Four sat across the room from us, out of hearing range. After a lesson on Van Gogh and his "Starry Night," Mrs. Baxter instructed us on how to use his painting as inspiration to create a night sky of our own. I chose to imagine a night sky over the island in my language arts project. After awhile Mrs. Baxter told us we could talk quietly while we sketched. Heather leaned over to me.

"Gwen, I didn't lose my language arts notebook."

"I didn't think you did."

"I unloaded my backpack at my desk and then went to my cubby to stuff it in. When I got back, everything was there but my notebook."

Heather spoke with her head close to mine as she watched the Foxfield Four who eyed us like a line-up of vultures.

"It was the last thing I pulled out so it was right on top. I spent a lot of time on it, Gwen. I feel awful."

"I believe you, Heather."

Hermy leaned forward.

"I came in a little later than usual today. You remember, Gwen; we came in at about the same time."

"That's right; we talked at our cubbies."

"So by the time I got to our cluster, Heather, you must have already left for the Lost and Found. If I had been on time, I might have noticed something."

"It's certainly not your fault, Hermy."

Heather reached into her jeans pocket.

"I didn't tell Mrs. Patterlin, but I found this note on the top shelf of my cubby this morning. It was done on a computer."

The note had been folded over and over again into a one-inch square. Heather slid it to me along the table. I turned my back to the rest of the class and pulled the note into my lap. My eyes widened as I read the word "TRAITOR" in the center of the square.

"Class, attention please. Unfortunately we've run out of time today. Next class period you will start in on your sketch as soon as you arrive. I would like each of you to put your Van Gogh sketch into your art folder in the file box by the window.

I quickly stuffed the note into my pocket. My stomach churned and my eye began to twitch. Poor Heather. I decided to read the note during restroom break.

"Gwen, here's a folder I've created for you."

Heather touched my arm. "Gwen, Mrs. Baxter is talking to you."

"I'm sorry, Mrs. Baxter," I replied quietly. "I didn't hear you."

"Here's a folder I've created for you," Mrs. Baxter repeated in a kind voice.

I stood and walked toward Mrs. Baxter. My stomach still churned and my eye still twitched. She leaned down and looked me straight in the eye. "Are you feeling okay, Gwen?"

"I'm fine, Mrs. Baxter. Thank you." I took my folder and returned to my seat.

My little white lie needed to be told. I glanced toward Olivia's table to see them all staring at me. If Heather hadn't had to defend me at the drinking fountain, none of this would have happened. Now I had to deal with the Foxfield Four who were getting revenge not only on me, but on Heather too for being my friend. What a mess.

"Tables 1-3, please put your sketches into your folders and line up. When tables 1-3 are done, tables 4-6 may do the same."

"I'm scared, Gwen," Heather whispered to me as we lined up at the door. "I'm usually not freaked out by stuff like this. Wait until you read the note."

Pretending to be brave, I whispered back, "Don't worry; we'll get to the bottom of this."

Chapter 22
The Nasty Note

Cluster 3 returned from the restroom. The M&M's and the rest of the cluster scurried to their seats like a group of pigeons hurrying to snatch up a crumb. Although they were separate people, the M&M's and Olivia and Amanda all looked the same. They dressed alike and even wore their hair almost the same. I wondered if one of them could do anything without the other. I never wanted to be that way. What a bore. How would you ever find out who you really were or what you could do by yourself?

"Maggie and Molly, this is not free time; you have an assignment to complete. Sam will explain it to you." Sam really knew her stuff when it came to reading and writing. Heather told me that Sam had won a contest in <u>Kids Write Magazine</u> for a story she wrote in third grade.

In unison the M&M's looked up and said, "Yes, Mrs. Patterlin."

"Cluster 2, you may take your restroom break."

Finally I would have a chance to read the note. I hurried down the hall and into the girls' room before Olivia. Luckily the last stall was still open; I slid the latch shut. Quickly retrieving the note from my pocket, I began reading.

Hey, Traitor- Remember Benedict Arnold, the traitor we learned about in Social Studies? He was punished for betraying his country. You betrayed us by being friends with our enemy. If you continue, you will be punished too. By the way if you tell anyone about this note, things will only get worse.

The Foxfield Four

My mind spun and my thoughts whizzed past each other like meteors in a meteor storm. How dare someone threaten Heather? Stuffing the note into my pocket, I hurried back to 25. Putting on my best acting face, I entered the room. Heather looked up at me and I smiled trying to act as normal as possible. Olivia, right on my heels, shoved me into Heather's desk.

"You're always in the way, Claire. Why don't you go back where you came from?"

"Shut up, Olivia. And mind your own business." I spoke as quietly as I could so Mrs. Patterlin wouldn't hear.

"I am minding my own business. Now move over and mind yours." Immediately changing the look on her face to a fake sweet smile, she bent over and looked Heather directly in the eyes. "Heather, I want you to sit with me at lunch today. I think it would be the smart thing to do."

Heather just stared back at Olivia.

"Miss Claire and Miss Roberts, please take your seats and begin reading. I don't recall giving anyone permission to speak."

It wasn't even lunchtime and already Mrs. Patterlin was not happy with my behavior. I headed for my seat. Olivia wiggled into hers making sure that everyone noticed her. I would have to put up with sitting next to her at least for awhile. Asking to have my seat moved so soon probably wouldn't be such a good idea.

Andrew looked at me, rolled his eyes, and shook his head. I started to dig through my desk for my reading book when I noticed that he had my book on his desk. He slid it over to me. While giving him a questioning look, I opened to the assigned page. Tucked inside the seam between pages 54 and 55, sat a tiny note flat out that read in the tiniest of print "Was the note to Heather bad? Just nod." I nodded trying not to be seen by anyone. The note continued. "I stayed here during break time and when you were gone, Amanda and the M&M's were passing notes. Something is definitely going on." I nodded again, scrunched up his note and quickly slipped it into my pocket. Luckily, during this whole time, Olivia had her back to me and was reading with the book in her lap. I tried to focus on "The Hare and the Tortoise," but my mind drifted. Hermy's Fruit Chewies practically stuck in my throat as time slowly made its way to Language Arts and the escape to my island.

Chapter 23
A Slip and Fall

Three claps echoed in room 25.

"Class, snack time is now over. All garbage should be neatly thrown into the trashcan. Please place any remaining food that you would like to save into your lunch bags. Hermy, stop eating now and do what I have instructed. Richie, get a wet paper towel and clean up the cracker crumbs from under your desk. While you're at it, also pick up all the papers and pencils on the floor around your desk. I believe I see the morning work you were looking for under your left foot. Cluster captains, please inspect the area around your cluster to make sure it is cleaned up before we begin Language Arts. I will count to twenty and by the time I am finished I expect the floor and desks to be clean and everyone should have his or her language arts notebook on his or her desks. Ready . . . one, two . . ."

Mrs. Patterlin counted slowly as everyone scrambled to get ready. Olivia, today's "cluster captain," took her job very seriously, shouting out orders like a drill sergeant.

"Andrew, there's a crumb of something gross right under your chair. It looks like broccoli. Did you actually have broccoli for a snack? How gross. I'd die if I had to eat broccoli for a snack."

"Then maybe you should try some," Andrew answered with a smirk.

Olivia stomped her foot and turned to her next victim.

Andrew picked up the remnant of his snack and tossed it out. Most of the time Andrew's way of dealing with Olivia was to ignore her, but even Andrew was getting fed up.

I was next in line for inspection. Olivia rounded the cluster and "accidentally" shoved my language arts notebook and all the stuff on top of my desk onto the floor. I looked up into her hateful face.

"Oops. Sorry, Gwendolyn. Maybe you should keep your stuff further in from the edge of your desk. You'd better pick it up before I have to report your mess to Mrs. Patterlin." Olivia's piercing blue eyes added an exclamation point to her words.

Staying out of trouble was not going to be easy today. While trying not to react to Miss Congeniality, I grit my teeth and almost wore off a layer of enamel. I bent over to pick up my papers lying at Olivia's feet and she struck again by stepping on my hand and pressing down hard. That was it. Reacting to the pain, I immediately pulled out my hand. Olivia lost her balance and landed in Hermy's lap. Hermy reacted as any warm-blooded fifth grade American boy would and stood up quickly to send Olivia straight to the floor. During this chain of events, the rest of the class completely lost it (except for the rest of the Four who didn't dare) and began teasing Olivia and Hermy about, well, you know, "liking each other."

Brushing off her denim mini-skirt, Olivia huffed to her feet. Her face, the color of a ripe radish, turned to me and only mouthed the words, "Just wait, Claire." Mrs. Patterlin flew over.

"Miss Roberts, what on earth do you think you are doing?"

Olivia just stood there with her mouth in a pout.

"You were asked to perform your duty as a cluster captain and instead I find you disturbing your fellow classmates and making a spectacle of yourself."

"But, Mrs. Patterlin, I . . ." was all she managed to spit out.

"I don't want to hear a word out of you, Miss Roberts. Now get yourself together and behave like a proper fifth grader and not a kindergartener."

Miracles do happen. Mrs. Patterlin continued to scold Olivia. I looked over at Heather whose mouth hung open in disbelief. Somehow though, I knew that Heather or I would pay for Olivia's embarrassment. When Mrs. Patterlin turned away, Olivia met my eyes and whispered, "I'll get you for this, Claire."

During all of the commotion, Hermy, very embarrassed and almost crying, flailed his arms as he pleaded with everyone to stop teasing him about Olivia.

"Come on, guys; leave me alone. It was an accident. You know I hate Olivia."

"Hermy, stop waving your arms like a windmill, be quiet, and settle down immediately. I don't know exactly what your part was in all of this, but I want it to end right now; do you hear me?"

"But Mrs. Patterlin . . . ."

"No more, Hermy. Do you understand?"

"Yes, Mrs. Patterlin. Sorry, Mrs. Patterlin."

Poor Hermy. He plopped into his chair, lifted the lid of his desk, slid his head in like a turtle, and pretended to fumble for some papers. I felt just awful for him. He had just been in the wrong place at the wrong time. And that wrong place just happened to be right behind Olivia.

"For the remainder of Language Arts, I do not want to hear a word from anyone. The only sounds I do want to hear are pen on paper and the turning of pages as you continue to work on your island project. Is that clear, Hermy?"

Hermy, with his head still in his desk, mumbled, "Yes, Mrs. Patterlin."

"Olivia?"

"Yes, Mrs. Patterlin."

Olivia quickly took her seat and opened her notebook.

"You're dead meat, Claire," she muttered under her breath.

Thirty minutes until lunch and a chance to regroup with Heather, Andrew and Hermy. As I pulled out my notebook, I glanced over to Heather who exchanged worried looks with me. I needed a break and writing always made me feel better. An escape to my island was just what I needed.

Chapter 24
A Brief Escape

About five minutes later a bell sounded in the hall. Heather popped up and slowly opened the door. Two shadows, made by the skylight in the hall ceiling, gradually moved into view. In the entrance to our room stood none other than Olivia and Amanda. Heather stepped back.

"Olivia, Amanda, what are you two doing here?" Heather looked at me and then back at the girls.

"Gwendolyn invited us, of course," sneered Olivia. Olivia's poison flowed out with her words.

Heather's eyes widened as she slowly turned her head toward me.

"You invited <u>them</u>?"

I nodded.

"See, Heather, we were invited just like you." Olivia smiled her snaky smile. "Oh, by the way, it must have been a little tricky to get here without a map."

"<u>You</u> took the map?"

"But I left enough copies for everyone," I insisted.

"Amanda and I thought it would be fun to see how clever the others were in finding your cottage without a map; didn't we Amanda?"

Amanda nodded while looking at the floor.

Heather turned and walked toward the window. She stared out without speaking.

I started to think that my inviting Olivia and Amanda might have been a mistake, but I couldn't change my decision now. I tried to lighten things up a bit.

"Did you see your room? It's right down the landing. I think you'll like it."

"No, not yet," replied Olivia. "We wanted to check in with our hostess first. Right, Amanda?"

Amanda just nodded again without saying a word.

"We didn't want to be rude."

"Right," I thought in my head.

"Well, how about you two just settle in and then we'll meet for supper later?"

"No thank you. We've already eaten. In fact we left some lunch for you downstairs. We'll just put our things in our room and explore the amusement park a bit. Is that alright with you, Gwen?"

"Absolutely, go ahead. We'll see you later."

"Sure, later. Hope to see you later too, Heather." Olivia called over her shoulder.

Heather didn't respond.

"Attention, everyone. Please close your notebooks; slide them into your desks; and get ready for lunch." Mrs. Patterlin's voice ignited in my ears and sped me back to room 25 in a hurry.

Chapter 25
Another Attack

Olivia hurried to slide in behind Heather in line. As we neared the cafeteria, she leaned forward to whisper in Heather's ear and as Heather shook her head "no," Olivia's knuckles pushed into the small of Heather's back. Heather winced, but didn't say anything. I felt like skipping ahead and punching Olivia in the face. Would Heather follow Olivia's "orders" and sit with the Foxfield Four?

As we entered the cafeteria, the smell of pizza, pbj's, and miscellaneous trapped odors from past lunches met our noses. Eating was the last thing on my mind. Kids hurried to claim their favorite spots. Heather, smiling, stood between the tables and waited for me to catch up with her.

"Well, Gwen, should we sit with Andrew and Hermy?"

"What about Olivia?"

"What about Olivia? You don't think that I'm about to listen to her, do you? Come on."

"You're incredible, Heather."

"I brought, did you?"

I lifted my lunch bag. Olivia and the girls needed to squeeze by in order to line up for hot lunch. They stopped directly in front of us and Olivia dropped a paper at Heather's feet. Olivia pointed to the filthy, tiled floor.

"Oh, look, Heather; you must have dropped something," Olivia added.

"It's against school rules to litter, Olivia." I said looking her straight in the eye. I bent to pick up the paper and as I did I felt a push from behind. Before I knew it, I was flat out on the floor. I jumped to my feet, brushed myself off, and turned to see Amanda with raised eyebrows and an innocent look on her face staring back at me.

"Oh, dear, Gwen, are you alright? You must have slipped on something."

The Foxfield Four snickered in unison.

"Maybe you should be more careful, Gwen," Olivia smirked. "You could get hurt."

Heather stepped up to face Olivia nose to nose. "Why don't you and your friends go to get your lunches, Olivia. You've done enough already."

"Hey look, girls. Miss Heather is defending her new little friend. How cute. Come on; let's go. It's starting to smell around here." The Foxfield Four pushed past us and got into line.

Mrs. Lucente, the teacher's assistant, hurried over.

"Are you hurt, Gwen? Some of the other kids said Amanda pushed you."

Now was my chance to tell an adult. Mrs. Lucente seemed really nice and so did Mrs. Foster, the other teacher's assistant. No. Heather and I needed to settle this by ourselves. Who knows what the Foxfield Four would do next if we said a word?

"No, I'm not hurt, Mrs. Lucente. I'm just so clumsy. I stooped to pick up a piece of paper and I must have slipped on someone's leftover sandwich or something. Just last week I slipped and fell in gym class. Really, it was all my fault. I'm just naturally clumsy, I guess."

I sounded ridiculous.

"Okay, dear, but remember, if you change your mind and want to talk later, you know where to find me."

"Thanks, Mrs. Lucente. I'm fine. Just a little embarrassed, that's all."

Mrs. Lucente walked away, but I felt that she didn't believe me. I hated lying, but I didn't want Heather to get into even more trouble with Olivia.

As Heather and I walked to our table, I realized that I was still clutching the piece of paper. I kept it hidden until we slid into our seats.

"Boy, what jerks they are." Hermy spouted.

"We saw everything," Andrew added.

"It's bad alright," I answered. "Keep an eye out for them, will you, guys?"

"We've got you covered."

Hermy nodded.

I turned to Heather.

"Here's the paper I picked up off the floor. It's another note." The tightly wrapped square looked just like the first one.

"Do you still have the other one?"

"Yes, it was awful."

"Hold on to it. Give me the new note."

Reluctantly, I placed the note in Heather's hand. As she turned it over, the blood rushed from her face. The lone word "TRAITOR" (this time in messy pencil) met her eyes. Heather started to unfold the note.

"Witches, Inc. is returning," Andrew quickly whispered.

Since their table was only a few feet from ours, the Foxfield Four had a clear view of us. I bent over, pretending to pick up something, and quickly whispered to Heather.

"Wait. Don't open it now. Act normal."

"Here, you take the note, Gwen. Mrs. Patterlin usually calls cluster 1 last. You can read it first and slip it to me when you come back from break; that way we'll both get a chance to see it."

I took the note and quickly shoved it into my front pocket.

We managed to down our lunches while trying to have an ordinary conversation with Andrew and Hermy. The vultures sat ready to swoop down at any moment.

Chapter 26
Cruel Code

Olivia rushed back from break before I had hardly entered the girls' room. When I closed the door to the last stall, I knew why she had been in such a rush. Smeared in lip-gloss on the back of the door were these letters: HS + GC, U R D-D.FF.I shivered. It didn't take a decoding genius to figure out the message. Knowing I didn't have much time, I quickly pulled out the latest note and with sweaty hands hurried to unfold it. The scribbled, penciled note screamed out its message in caps:

> *H.*
> *NOT JOINING US FOR LUNCH*
> *WAS A BIG MISTAKE.*
> *YOU'D BETTER BE CAREFUL.*
> *TOO BAD ABOUT YOUR NOTEBOOK.*
> *IS G.C.WORTH IT?*
> *F.F.*

Trembling, I folded the note into a tiny square, hid it in the palm of my hand, and left. Heather needed to read the note before recess and I needed to tell her to look in the last stall during break. Thinking quickly, I came up with a plan. I remembered the small brush in my back pocket. I would carry it into the room, accidentally drop it on the floor by Heather's desk, stoop to pick it up, slip her the note, and tell her to look in the last stall.

As I looked down the hall, something I hadn't counted on happened. Mrs. Patterlin stood staring at me like one of the concrete lions in front of the New York Public Library.

"Miss Claire, is everything alright? You took longer than usual in the girls' room today."

"I'm fine, thank you, Mrs. Patterlin. I just have a little stomach ache, that's all."

"Okay, then; take your seat."

Whew. That worked out okay.

While Mrs. Patterlin walked a few steps past me down the hall to check on stragglers, I carried out my plan.

"Use the last stall," I whispered to Heather as I slid the note to her and picked up my brush.

"Why?" She whispered back.

"You'll see."

Upon arriving at my cluster, I discovered that my pen and pencil tray was totally empty except for a huge wad of pink bubble gum, still wet. "I wonder who did that," my brain asked sarcastically. Andrew didn't see anything because he was in the boys' room and Jackie, my other cluster mate, always used her spare minutes to sketch in her sketchpad. Olivia, the obvious culprit, pretended to be completely engrossed in the new reading assignment. I breathed a deep sigh, scooped up the gum with a tissue, threw it out, took my seat, and opened my reading book. I stared at the words on page sixty-seven; nothing registered in my brain. It was very, very hard to sit next to Olivia.

"And last, Cluster 1; you may leave for the restrooms."

Heather glanced toward me as she left the room.

Chapter 27
Dampened Plans

Mrs. Patterlin counted heads.

"We're missing someone."

"It's Heather, Mrs. Patterlin. She's still in the girls' room. Would you like me to get her?"

"That would be fine, Gwendolyn. The two of you may then meet the class outside for recess. If there is a problem, I'll be in the copy room."

"Yes, Mrs. Patterlin."

As I left the line to go down the hall, Andrew, who was immediately in front of me, turned and grabbed my arm.

"Meet Hermy and me out on the playground. We'll be behind the large slides near the fence. Heather knows where."

"Okay." Trying not to look panicky, I walked normally down the hall, but as soon as the class rounded the corner I picked up speed. I entered the girls' room. It looked empty. I checked for feet under the stall doors.

"Heather? Are you here? Heather?"

"Gwen, is that you?" A small voice echoed from the last stall.

"Yes, it's me. Come on out. The class already went outside for recess."

I heard feet hit the floor and the door to the last stall opened. Heather, her face tear-stained, slowly walked toward me.

"It's getting worse, Gwen. I thought it was bad last year, but it's getting worse."

"What do you mean, last year?"

"Remember in gym yesterday when you said that you had made a mess of things and I started to say something but stopped?"

"Yes."

"Well, this whole thing with Olivia goes way back."

"Come on, Heather, you can fill me in on the way out. We'll be noticed if we don't show up soon. Andrew said to meet him and Hermy behind the big slides. He said you would know where."

"Okay."

As we stepped into the hall, we heard kids screaming and laughing. Without a warning, the dark sky had opened up and poured down buckets of rain. Drenched by the sudden deluge, fifth graders, spilling into the hallway, looked like wet puppies trying to shake dry after unwanted baths.

"We'll have to talk later," I whispered.

Chapter 28
The Plot Thickens

"Girls and boys, today we're going to combine language arts with cursive. I want you to continue your stories making sure that you use your best cursive writing. We will work until 2:30, take a short break, and then have our spelling test."

A few groans shot out from various clusters.

"You didn't think that I'd forgotten about the spelling test, did you?" Mrs. Patterlin asked with a smile.

No, I didn't think that Mrs. Patterlin ever forgot spelling tests or anything else for that matter. Wow, a whole half-hour to get back to the island. Olivia had been strangely quiet since returning from recess. I wondered why, but couldn't think about it right now. Let's see; where did I leave off?

Heather didn't respond.

Okay, so Heather was upset. (The one thing that I really liked about writing was being in control of what happened. Real life doesn't work that way.) Let's see. What should I have happen next? Heather needs to say something.

I closed the door and leaned on it. Heather turned toward me.

"I can't believe that you actually invited Olivia and Amanda for the summer. They'll only cause trouble."

"I'm sorry, Heather, but I just thought that maybe if they got to know me better that we could actually become friends."

"That's a nice thought, but I doubt that things will turn out the way that you want."

"It seems that you know a lot more about them that you haven't told me yet."

"Olivia and I go way back to when we both attended Foxfield Primary. We were actually friends until everything changed."

"What happened?"

"It's a long story. Why don't we go downstairs and get something to eat while the deadly duo is out. If you like I can start to fill you in then."

Just then I realized that my story needed some information that I didn't have yet. Heather had never told me what had gone wrong between Olivia and her. I mean it was obvious that Heather was nothing like Olivia. I wondered how Heather would have had Olivia for a friend in the first place. Maybe Olivia wasn't always mean and nasty. There were too many unanswered questions. I decided to keep writing, but not to include the part about Heather's and Olivia's friendship breaking up.

"Nice job, everyone." Mrs. Patterlin put an end to our writing with her booming voice and I realized that I had spent most of my time thinking and not writing. "All of you used good posture and from what I observed, most of you seem to be moving forward quite well on your writing. Remember: the most important thing is to use your imagination and let your story flow out. We'll worry about fixing your grammar and spelling mistakes at a later date. Relax and have fun. Are there any questions before we have our spelling test?"

I raised my hand.

"Yes, Gwendolyn?"

"Is there any word limit? I mean, can we write as much as we like? I think mine is going to be pretty long."

"No, no word limit. That reminds me. Heather, did your language arts notebook turn up yet?"

"No, Mrs. Patterlin."

"Has anyone seen Heather's notebook or does anyone have any idea where it might have gone?"

Olivia jutted her arm into the air.

"Yes, Livi?"

"I think that Heather *thinks* that she brought it to school, but she probably didn't. She must have been careless and didn't actually pack her notebook."

"No, Olivia, you're wrong. I am not careless. I did pack my notebook and I unpacked it here this morning, as you well know." Heather's strong voice supported her words.

"If there's one thing that Heather isn't; it's careless," Andrew added while looking straight at Olivia.

"You go, Andrew." I thought to myself.

"I've known Heather for a long time and she's never been careless with anything."

Anticipating an argument, clusters started to wiggle and buzz.

"Thank you, Andrew and Livi, for your opinions. I'm sure that Heather's notebook will be found. We'll all keep an eye out for it."

Mrs. Patterlin turned to Heather. "My dear, I know this is upsetting to you, but it will all work out. You are a very responsible young lady and I'm sure that your notebook has somehow just been misplaced. Maybe someone picked it up by mistake. At the end of the day, during free time, we'll all clean out our desks. Perhaps it will show up then. Right now, everyone please take out a piece of loose-leaf paper, fold it vertically, place your name and the date in your best cursive on the top line and number from 1-5 in the first column and 6-10 in the second column. Your spelling test will begin in exactly 30 seconds."

As we readied our papers, I wondered if the notebook would turn up during clean out. Olivia or Amanda or one of the M&M's certainly had the notebook hidden. I would have to watch them closely. They might try to hide it somewhere else in the room or worse yet throw it in the garbage. I'm sure that Heather, Andrew, and Hermy were thinking the same thing. With all of us on the lookout, we were sure to get to the truth. Right now I had a spelling test to think about.

Chapter 29
The Set-up

"Mrs. Patterlin. Oh, Mrs. Patterlin. I have a question, Mrs. Patterlin." Benny's hand waved in the air as he stood with his right knee on his chair and his left foot on the floor. "Excuse me, Mrs. Patterlin."

"Benny, you know that calling my name and waving your arm in the air is not the proper way to get my attention. Please sit in your seat, raise your hand and quietly wait to be called upon."

Benny did as he was told, but it was too late; the class was already giggling.

Mrs. Patterlin pointed to Benny.

"Yes, Benny. Do you have an important question to ask before we begin the spelling test?"

"Yes, Mrs. Patterlin."

"Well, what is it?"

"Well, you see, Mrs. Patterlin; I didn't have time to study last night because of basketball tryouts and I didn't get home until late and Mom made me go to bed right away. Do I still have to take the test today?"

"Benny, I'm sorry that you didn't get a chance to study last night, but isn't it true that you've had the word list for a week?"

"Yes, well, sort of, Mrs. Patterlin. I mean I didn't really have my list for a week. My mom always empties out my backpack and I think she threw it out with the rest of my papers."

"Benny, it's a fifth grader's responsibility, not his mother's, to make sure a spelling list is kept in a safe place, now isn't it?"

"Yes, Mrs. Patterlin."

"The answer to your question, Benny, is 'yes.' Yes, you still have to take the test today. Now finish getting your spelling paper ready. Do the best that you can."

During lunch Andrew had given me an update on some of the kids. He said that Benny has a lot of trouble with his schoolwork especially spelling, but he really likes science. Andrew and Benny were partners for the electricity unit in third grade; Benny just loved it. He finished all the experiments before everyone else and even got an A on the final test. Miss Henderson, their third grade teacher, even had Benny go over the answers on his test with the rest of the class. Benny had been so proud that day.

"We'll see how you do and then talk about it later. Okay, Benny?" Mrs. Patterlin smiled.

"Okay, Mrs. Patterlin." Benny smiled back.

I liked Mrs. Patterlin. She was hard, but also fair. I think she remembered what it was like to be a kid even though she was probably as old as Grammie.

Olivia shifted her chair closer to mine. Now what? I didn't want to make a scene so I just pretended that it didn't happen. The spelling test began.

"#1 is winning. Winning a game is a wonderful feeling, but being a good teammate is even a better feeling. Winning."

"#2 is entering. While entering the house, Mother smelled smoke coming from the kitchen. Entering."

"#3 is their. Now listen carefully to the sentence, boys and girls; that will tell you which 'their' I mean. The boys left their ball on the field and would have to retrieve it after school. Their."

Olivia shifted even closer and this time she tilted her head in my direction. She was cheating off my paper. I moved it to the left and tried to block my area with my right shoulder.

"Miss Claire, is there a problem?"

"No, Mrs. Patterlin."

"Then could you face forward please?"

Feeling my face redden, I turned to face front. Olivia didn't stop.

"#4 is there. Listen carefully now. I left your paper over there on my desk so it wouldn't get lost. There."

I wrote "there" as small as I could and tried to cover the left side of my paper so that Olivia couldn't see my first column of words, but it didn't stop her. She looked at my paper just when Mrs. Patterlin looked somewhere else.

"#5 is they're. Ready? They're going to try to get to the movies tonight if the tickets aren't sold out. They're."

I knew that I had kept the three words straight. When we got to #6, Olivia shifted back in her seat and suddenly didn't pay attention to me anymore. I glanced over and discovered why. Just under the bottom corner of her spelling test was a tiny cheat sheet. She needed me for "their, there, and they're" because she didn't know which was which, but she didn't need me for the other words because she had them in front of her. I hated cheaters, but what could I do? I hated tattle-talers too.

I concentrated on the rest of my words and then chose five to write creative sentences for on the back of the paper. Here's how they turned out:

1. If Julie and her friend knew sign <u>language</u>, the boys couldn't figure out what they were saying.
2. Heather <u>wondered</u> if she would ever find her notebook.
3. Amanda tried to <u>hinder</u> the girl from moving down the aisle in the cafeteria by sticking out her foot.

4. Dealing with bullies is not a <u>minor</u> problem.
5. <u>Their</u> biggest mistake was letting <u>their</u> talkative friend in on <u>their</u> secret.

There, I was done. I checked over my paper and covered it until everyone finished.

"Attention, boys and girls; you should have completed your sentences by now and checked over your papers. Cluster captains, please collect the papers from your cluster."

Olivia, our illustrious cluster captain, circled like a bird of prey and took each of our tests. I watched her as she brought them up to Mrs. Patterlin. After she handed them over, she whispered something in Mrs. Patterlin's ear and pointed to me while handing her another slip of paper.

"Miss Claire, may I see you for a moment please?"

I approached Mrs. Patterlin.

Chapter 30
Take Two

"Gwendolyn, let's step out in the hall for a moment."

When a teacher asks you to step out in the hall, it's not a good sign. I remembered Olivia's pointing her finger at me and I remembered the slip of paper. My worst fears surfaced to the top of my brain.

"Class, I expect you to behave as if I were right in front of you and watching you prepare your things for dismissal. Do not forget to take a copy of your new spelling list from the table. Right, Benny? Put your daily notes into your take home folders. Remember: cubbies should be left empty. Also, while cleaning out your desks, check to see if Heather's notebook ended up in your desk by mistake. I will return in a few minutes."

I stood like a naughty puppy next to Mrs. Patterlin. Heather looked worried for me. Most everyone else just stared. I wondered if Heather's notebook would "turn up" during clean-out. Andrew, Hermy and Heather would have to keep their eyes wide open.

The door closed behind us. Foxfield classrooms vibrated with the excitement of the end of the day while I stood on a guillotine before my executioner. Mrs. Patterlin handed me the piece of paper.

"Miss Claire, do you know anything about this?"

It was Olivia's cheat sheet.

"It's not mine, Mrs. Patterlin." I tried not to tattle, but I wanted to tell the truth.

"Are you sure, Miss Claire? Olivia says she found it on the floor near your desk as she was picking up the spelling papers."

"I'm sure it's not mine, Mrs. Patterlin. Spelling is easy for me and even if it weren't, I still wouldn't use a cheat sheet."

"Do you know whose paper this might be?"

I didn't want to lie, but if I told on Olivia, she might get revenge. I decided to tell Mrs. Patterlin the simple truth.

"Yes, Mrs. Patterlin. I know whose paper it might be."

"Well?"

"But I can't tell you because then I would be a tattle-taler."

"I see."

We both stood there while the end of the day came fast.

"What do you think I should do about this?"

My first impulse was to say "I don't know," but then inspiration struck like lightning.

"Olivia found the note, Mrs. Patterlin. Why don't you see if she has any ideas about it? If she doesn't, then maybe the two of us could take the spelling test over again right now. We're the only two involved. She found the note and it was near *my* desk that is right next to hers. We still have a few minutes left until dismissal."

"That's an excellent idea, Gwendolyn."

By giving Mrs. Patterlin my suggestion, I felt that I let her know what I was thinking without really saying exactly what I was thinking.

Mrs. Patterlin opened the door and told me to get ready for dismissal while she talked to Olivia. The door shut again and in a few moments opened to reveal a very unhappy Olivia who skulked over to her desk.

"Class, for the last few minutes of the day, I would like all of you to take out your library books and read silently while I give Gwendolyn and Olivia their spelling tests again."

Benny waved his arm in the air, but actually waited to be called upon.

"Yes, Benny, what is it?"

"Why do they have to take it over again?"

"That's none of your business; now is it, Benny?"

"No, Mrs. Patterlin." Benny's face twisted into a weird smirk.

"Now do what you were told to do, Benny."

"Yes, Mrs. Patterlin."

Olivia and I sat at opposite ends of the long, rectangular worktable like two rivals about to wage battle. Mrs. Patterlin gave us each a clean sheet of paper and told us to prepare it for a spelling test. Standing tall between us, she dictated the words in new sentences and in a different order and told us we wouldn't have to write sentences this time. Remembering the order of there, their, and they're from the last test wouldn't help Olivia. Confident that the truth would come out, I handed my paper to Mrs. Patterlin. Olivia followed with hers.

By the time we had finished, Mr. Turner's voice, delivering the order of the buses, was booming over the loudspeaker. "First dismissal." That was me. As I passed Heather's cluster and said goodbye, she handed me a note. I wondered if anything had happened or "shown up" during clean-out. Clutching the note in my hand, I smiled, nodded, and hurried down the hall. The day could have ended in disaster, but it didn't. I felt like a pitcher on the verge of striking out the last hitter in the ninth inning. The new spelling test would reveal my innocence. Hopefully, mighty Olivia would strike out. Unfortunately, there were probably many games yet to be played in a very difficult season.

Chapter 31
Family Fun

Mom and I walked out into the gorgeous fall day. The cloud burst during recess had ended as quickly as it had happened. The trees, just beginning to put on their autumn overcoats, stood tall against the turquoise sky. The early fall sun seemed to illuminate everything clearer than in the summer when it always seemed just a little hazy. The sun warmed my shoulders as the breeze cooled my face. It felt good to be going home.

"You seem to be happy today, honey. Did you have a good day?"

"Well, it ended up being a pretty good day."

I felt funny not telling Mom about the Foxfield Four. I still thought that Heather and I should handle them ourselves.

"Glad to hear it. I had a better day too. Hey, how about being really bad?"

"What do you mean?"

"Well, on my way over, I spotted an ice cream shop that advertised twenty-five flavors of soft ice cream. It's right on the way home."

"Ice cream before dinner? Really, Mom?"

"Why not? Grammie's coming over later and we should celebrate our move. I'm sure that you won't refuse pizza later on."

"Pizza?"

"Sure. Grammie will be here about 6:30. I thought we'd try out AJ's down the street from our house."

"Ice cream before dinner, Grammie, _and_ pizza? It doesn't get any better than this. Thanks, Mom."

As I hugged Mom I saw a paper drop to the sidewalk. With all this "good stuff" going on, I had almost forgotten that I had Heather's note in my hand. I grabbed it up and stuffed it in my pocket. As we hurried to the car, a small cloud made a shadow on the warm sidewalk and a shiver passed down my back.

Chapter 32
E-mail Exchange

Heather's note had only said, "Check your e-mail" so I wanted to do that first.

As we pulled up to our front door, I let Mom know my before-supper plans.

"First I'm going to check my e-mail, Mom."

"Okay, Honey, but make it quick. I'd like you to get your homework done before Grammie gets here."

"No problem. I just have to continue my island project and look over my new spelling words."

"Sounds good. I'll call you when she gets here. What kind of pizza do you want?"

"Gee, I'm so full of coconut ice cream, it's hard to think about pizza right now, but I guess I'll stick with the usual."

"Double cheese and pepperoni?"

"That's it. I think it's Grammie's favorite too. I hope AJ's is as good as Uncle Chop's Pizza back in Hartwick."

"Well, I don't know if that's possible, but it's worth a try."

"Mom, do you mind if I do my homework outside on the deck?"

"That's fine. Just let me know when you're heading out."

"I will."

I double-staired it up to my room and threw my backpack on the bed.

While I started up my computer, I pulled out Heather's e-mail address: _heathers@penme.net_. Mine is _gwenclaire@scribble2me.com_. The computer seemed to take forever to load. Okay, username: GwenC; password: coolwriter. There. I scanned my e-mail quickly: spam and lots of it, a message from Grammie, two from friends back at Hartwick and finally the e-mail from Heather. I double-clicked and pulled my chair closer to the desk.

Hi, Gwen. My notebook was "found" during clean-out in the mess on the floor. It was kicked over by my desk. The cover was torn and bent and my writing was all blurred with water smears. Scary stuff was scribbled across the pages. On one page it said, "Stay away from her, B——h, or you'll regret it." I'm really scared now, Gwen. I want to tell Mom and Dad, but I'm afraid it just might make things worse. We're leaving in a few minutes to go to my aunt's for the weekend and we won't get home until late on Sunday so I won't be able to check my e-mail. I'll see you Monday. We have to figure something out soon.

Your friend, Heather

P.S. Please don't tell your mom.

I printed a copy of the e-mail, stashed it in my "secret box" in the darkest corner of my closet, and deleted the original. I stood up and started pacing the floor. My stomach felt like it had been punched in a fight and my brain started up on high speed trying to figure out what to do. We had had an assembly on bullies at Hartwick last year, but I didn't really listen as hard as I should have because no bullies were bothering any of my friends or me. Now I wish that I had listened more closely. The Foxfield Four were bullies and had to be stopped. After pacing for a few minutes, I decided that I needed to relax. I looked over my new spelling list for a few minutes and then grabbed my language arts notebook and headed downstairs. Grammie would be here before I knew it and I'd have to act as if nothing were bothering me. Writing would help me relax.

"Mom, I'll be on the deck."

"Okay, honey." Mom's voice echoed from her room down the hall.

I grabbed my sweatshirt off the hook, pushed open the sliding doors, and nestled into the cushiony chair. I flipped through my notebook and found where I had left off.

"It's a long story. Why don't we go downstairs and get something to eat while the deadly duo is out. If you like I can start to fill you in then."

Oh, that's right, I didn't know what I needed to know for the Heather in the story to tell me about her friendship with Olivia. Just then inspiration struck. I knew what I needed to do.

As we hurried down the stairs to the kitchen, I realized that I hadn't investigated the amusement park yet. I couldn't wait to get there; especially with Heather along for the fun.

"You know what, Heather?"

"What?"

"Let's forget about Olivia and Amanda for awhile and get outside and look around. I can't wait to explore the amusement park. What do you think? We can get something to eat there. Let's have some fun."

"Sounds wonderful. Anyway, I wasn't about to eat anything that Olivia made. There's so much more, Gwen. Olivia and the Foxfield Four really scare me."

"Well, at least the M&M's aren't here. Come on. Let's forget about all of them for awhile."

We opened the door to find a carriage with a pink and purple canopy parked out front. We looked at each other and just giggled as we jumped in.

"To the amusement park, driver," I pretended to sound so grown-up.

"As you wish, ladies."

We were off.

The blue skies and island breezes made it a perfect weather day. Straight ahead down a wide, bumpy cobblestone path stood the highest riding wheel that I had ever seen.

"Stop here please, driver. Thank you for the ride. Come on, Heather, the wheel awaits us."

All the workers in the amusement park resembled the nicest adults that I had met in my life. In fact, the operator of the wheel looked like my Uncle John who died when I was little; I will never forget how sweet he was to me. He had baby bunnies in his backyard every spring and it was such a thrill to go out and try to find them. We never touched them, of course, but I will never forget how wonderful it was to see those little bundles of fur.

"Well, hello, Gwendolyn and Heather; my name is Jonathon. Are you ready for a ride?"

"Yes, sir," we answered in unison.

"A couple of your friends are already aboard," Jonathon added.

"Oh, no," I thought. Would we have to deal with Olivia and Amanda so soon?

Just then I heard the sliding doors open slowly behind me.

"Hey, you."

"Grammie!"

Chapter 33
Monday "Mourning"

The late bell sounded. Where on earth was Heather? My stomach bubbled like a witch's brew.

"Settle down, everyone. Please begin your morning work while I take attendance."

Concentrate on morning work without knowing where Heather was? Impossible.

"Our only absentee today is Heather. Does anyone ride her bus?"

Up shot Olivia's hand.

"I do, Mrs. Patterlin. Heather fell after she got off our bus this morning. She had to go to the nurse's office."

"Thank you, Livi. I'll call Mrs. Muller right now."

I hoped Heather was okay. Wait a minute. Olivia rode Heather's bus?

"Hello, Mrs. Muller? Yes, this is Mrs. Patterlin. Is Heather Sebastian with you? Oh, she is. Okay. Will she be returning to class or going home?"

I thought my brain would explode.

"Oh, I'm sorry to hear that."

Hear what?

"Yes, yes. Well, tell her to rest up. Okay, then. Thank you. Bye now."

Mrs. Patterlin walked back to her desk, wrote something on the attendance sheet, and placed it in the envelope on the door. During the phone conversation, Olivia didn't even lift her head from her math paper. Miss Busy Body acted like she wasn't interested. That was weird. I tried to begin my work, but just couldn't. Finally I stood up and went to Mrs. Patterlin's desk.

"Excuse me, Mrs. Patterlin."

"Yes, Gwendolyn."

"Is Heather okay?"

"Yes, dear. She bruised her knees quite badly on the concrete steps, but she'll be okay."

"Is she going home?"

"No, Gwen; Mrs. Muller took very good care of her. Don't worry, she'll be back here before we go to music class."

"Thank you, Mrs. Patterlin."

As I worked on my math, I couldn't help but be distracted by the news about Heather. I felt there was more to the story.

Time dragged on. We put the math problems on the board, and discussed each and every one in detail. The video on the rainforest in Social Studies interested me for a while until I spotted some note passing in the dark among the Foxfield Four. Mrs. Patterlin was correcting papers at her desk and didn't seem to notice what was happening.

"You shouldn't be passing notes, you know," I whispered to Olivia.

"Mind your own business, idiot," she whispered back. "Are you going to tell?"

Instead of saying another word, I grabbed the note from the floor as Olivia tried to slide it over to Amanda with her foot.

"Give that back," Olivia whispered urgently. "It's not yours."

Amanda stretched out of her seat without standing up and tried to get it back from me. Too late. I had shoved it into my desk.

All of a sudden the lights flashed on.

"Alright, class; we'll have to stop here for now. It's time for music so we'll finish the video when we return. Raise your hand if you like it so far."

Everyone's hand went up, everyone's except for Olivia's that is. Her face looked white with anger.

"Olivia, you are the only one that didn't raise her hand."

"What, Mrs. Patterlin?"

"I said that you were the only one that didn't raise her hand."

"Sorry, Mrs. Patterlin. Yes, I am buying hot lunch."

The room burst into laughter.

"Hot lunch? No, Livi Dear, I asked about hot lunch long ago. I asked if you liked the video."

Olivia's white face turned scarlet.

"Oh, sorry, Mrs. Patterlin. I guess that I didn't hear you. Sure, the video was great. Too bad it ended so soon."

Again the class started to roar.

"Olivia, we haven't finished watching it yet. We are going to finish it after music."

"Oh, yeah, right."

By this time Olivia was livid. Not only was she embarrassed, but also she knew that I had her precious note.

Just then my day improved; in walked Heather. She moved stiffly and it was clear that her knees really hurt.

"Welcome, Heather," said Mrs. Patterlin. "Are you feeling a little better?"

Heather nodded as she placed her jacket in her cubby and emptied her backpack. I gave her a little "thumbs-up" sign. She managed a weak smile as she slowly took her seat.

"That's good news. You're just in time for music."

As we prepared to line up, I reached into my desk to get the confiscated note. Olivia noticed what I was doing and reached in too. Luckily, I was quicker than she was, and grabbed it up. I immediately reached out my hand to Andrew who had witnessed the whole note-passing episode. He quickly snatched the note and stuffed it into his pocket. Olivia threw him a look that could kill an elephant.

"And last, but not least, Cluster 2 may line up."

Olivia, directly behind me in line, breathed down my neck. "You'd better get that note back and give it to me. It's none of your d—n business."

Swearing, huh? I decided then and there that the note must definitely be "my business."

Chapter 34
Mrs. Ray, Music

Mrs. Ray greeted us with a huge smile at the music room door. Her dark chocolate eyes peeked out from under her equally dark hair. She spoke to each of us as we entered her room and, of course, stopped when she got to me, the "new" kid.

"Well, whom do we have here?" Mrs. Ray's words sounded as sweet as warmed honey. I found out later from Heather that Mrs. Ray was originally from West Virginia.

"Good morning, Mrs. Ray. I'm Gwen."

"It's nice to meet you, Gwen. Welcome to music. I hope that you enjoy music."

"Oh, I do, Mrs. Ray."

"I saw on the interest survey that Gwen filled out at registration that she plays the piano," added Mrs. Patterlin.

"That's wonderful, Gwen. Have you played a long time?"

"Since I was six."

"Well, I'll have you play for us sometime. Come on in. Do you have a friend you'd like to sit next to today?"

"Yes, Heather."

"Go right ahead, dear; I know that it's hard being new to a school. I was in your situation several times when I was growing up. By the way, did you know that Heather is also a pianist?"

"No, I didn't." Wow, Heather played too.

I loved Mrs. Ray already. I wondered if it was too late to sign up for chorus. For that matter I wondered if she taught piano; I needed a new piano teacher. That would be so cool.

I quickly sat down next to Heather. This was our first chance to talk.

"Are you alright? How are your knees?"

"Really sore."

"How did you fall?"

"I sort of tripped up the stairs."

"Tripped up the stairs? How did that happen?"

"It's a long story that started when Olivia sat next to me on the bus."

"Olivia sat next to you? How scary is that?"

"I know. She was being really friendly too. I thought that maybe she was sorry for everything that had happened and was trying to make up."

"Fat chance."

"I know. Then, after a few minutes, she patted me on the back and went back to sit with Amanda."

"Patted you on the back?"

Heather nodded.

"Then what happened?"

"Nothing. At least not right away."

"How did you end up in the nurse's office?"

"It was stupid really."

"What do you mean?"

"Well, it seems that Olivia's pat on the back was really her way of sticking a sign to my sweater."

"A sign? What did it say?"

"It was a drawing of a heart and inside it said 'Heather loves Andrew.'"

"What a moron she is. Doesn't she have anything better to do? How did you find out it was there?"

"Well, after I got off the bus, I noticed kids were staring and pointing at me. I didn't know what was going on. I felt so embarrassed. Finally, Mrs. Baxter, who was on bus duty, noticed the sign, pulled it off my back, and asked me if I knew it was there."

"I could have died. I was so embarrassed that when I turned to go I actually tripped up the stairs and landed on my knees. My stuff scattered everywhere and my knees were a bloody mess."

"So that's how you ended up in the nurse's office."

Heather nodded.

"I didn't know that Olivia and Amanda lived on your bus route."

"We've lived down the street from each other since I moved here. That's how we first became friends. Even our mothers became friends."

"Okay, that explains the jealousy thing."

"What do you mean?"

"Well, it seems that if Olivia can't have you for a friend then no one else can. She's determined to make your life miserable."

"Well, so far her plan is working."

"I know. Plus there's a new note that I grabbed during the video. Andrew has it. Olivia's really on the warpath now. I'm afraid of what she'll do next."

Heather nodded and lowered her head.

"Alright, class. May I have your attention please?"

"Don't worry, Heather. We'll put an end to this bullying one way or another."

Music class just flew by. Last year's teacher used recordings instead of the piano and we only did songs from a really old and boring music book. Mrs. Ray played the piano beautifully and we did these neat rhythm exercises; plus, she split the room up into groups to sing different parts of some really cool songs.

As we lined up to leave, I whispered to Heather.

"I didn't know that you played piano."

"Sure. I've been taking piano lessons from Mrs. Ray since I moved to Foxfield."

"She's your piano teacher?"

"Yes, and she's the best."

"I play piano too and I need a teacher. I wonder if she has room for me."

"Well, she usually teaches two students at a time and the boy who was taking lessons with me just changed his lesson time so his spot is open. Wouldn't that be perfect?"

"I'm going to ask her right now."

We edged closer to Mrs. Ray as we headed out the door to meet Mrs. Patterlin.

"Excuse me, Mrs. Ray, but Heather and I were just talking about piano lessons. She said you might have an opening at her time."

"Yes, as a matter of fact I do, Gwen. Do you think that you might be interested?"

"I sure would."

Mrs. Ray took a slip of paper and a pen from her desk behind her.

"Write down your name and phone number and I'll call your mom to see if she agrees and if the time is right for both of you."

"Thanks, Mrs. Ray."

In spite of Heather's achy knees, we practically flew back to class. Little did we know what awaited us.

Chapter 35
Serious Trouble

"Attention, class. We will be finishing the video about rainforests very soon. Right now, I would like you all to take out your snacks and get ready to take turns going to the restroom. Cluster 2, you may leave quietly."

Olivia and I were the last to leave. Halfway down the hall, Olivia shoved me into the wall.

"Okay, Claire, I want the note back." Olivia whispered through her gritted teeth. The others had hurried ahead. We were alone in the empty hall.

"Let me go." Olivia, almost three inches taller than me, held me against the wall. I struggled to free myself. "I don't have it."

I didn't want to make a scene, but in a moment I might have to.

"I know that you don't have it, idiot. Andrew does. Get it back to me during the video or you'll be sorry."

With one final shove, Olivia released me and turned to go. I decided to take my time by the drinking fountain until I saw her returning to the room. I wasn't about to get stuck alone with her in the girls' room. The hall had been bad enough.

After leaving the girls' room, the Foxfield Four ringleader hurried to the classroom; luckily, she hadn't turned to see me by the fountain.

"Hurry up, Gwen. You'll drink up the whole reservoir."

Startled, I jumped up and almost bumped Andrew in the mouth.

"Get your drink; then I have to tell you something." I stepped aside while he took a long drink.

"What's the matter?"

"Do you still have the note?"

"Oh, yeah, sure; I'd almost forgotten about it. Here it is." Andrew pulled it from his pocket just as Mrs. Patterlin stepped into the hallway.

"Boys and girls, let's hurry along now."

Andrew passed the note to me as we moved quickly toward the room. I slipped it into my pocket. As we came in, Heather looked up. I bit my lip and shook my head in a way that warned her not to say anything just now.

After everyone had returned from the restrooms, Mrs. Patterlin started up the video and turned off the lights. We could finish our snacks while we watched and could only get up to throw out garbage.

"Remember what I said, Claire," Olivia glared at me and then turned toward the TV.

Fortunately, the TV was set up so that the only way that Olivia could see it would be to have her back to me. I figured she probably would pay close attention to the video especially after that incident with Mrs. Patterlin before music. If I were careful, I could read the note and then hand it over to Heather while throwing out my garbage by the door near where she sat.

A little way into the video during an interesting part about the snakes of the rainforest, I made my move. Slowly reaching into my back pocket, I pulled out the note and carefully unfolded it in my lap.

Hey, girls-
It seems that "signs" point to the fact that my plan
worked out even better than I expected. Ha. Ha.
Poor little H. — she'll learn who is in control
around here and who she should hang around with.
If not, then we'll have to try something else.
Stay with me, girls; the Foxfield Four will soon be the Foxfield Five.
O.

I started to think about the notes as evidence, evidence that the Foxfield Four was a group of bullies that needed to be stopped.

Trying to act as normal as possible, I folded up the note and picked up the wrapper from my fruit strips; I then casually headed toward the wastebasket. I slipped the note onto Heather's desk, dropped off the garbage and went back to my seat. Looking over my shoulder, I watched as Heather read the note. Even in the dark, I could tell that she had turned pale. After stuffing the note in her pocket, she put her head down on her desk.

Chapter 36
The Worried Wait

As the video ended, Heather lifted her head off the desk and raised her hand.

"Yes, Heather."

"Mrs. Patterlin, could I go to the nurse's office? I'm not feeling so well."

"Of course, Heather. Gwendolyn, could you please accompany Heather?"

"Sure, Mrs. Patterlin."

"I'll call ahead and let Mrs. Muller know you're coming. I hope you feel better, dear."

We stepped into the hall. Heather leaned on my arm as we slowly headed toward Mrs. Muller's office.

"Heather, I'm so worried. Are you going to be all right?"

"Don't worry, Gwen. I'll be okay. My knees are throbbing and that note kind of made my stomach queasy. I just need some rest."

"What you need is to stop being bullied."

Just then Mrs. Muller met us in the hall and took Heather by the arm.

"Thank you, Gwen. I'll take care of Heather now."

"Bye, Heather. I'll talk to you later."

"Bye, Gwen."

Heather still had the latest note in her pocket. If her mom were like mine, she would probably check the pockets before putting the jeans in the wash. I didn't want to tell anyone yet. I guess I was afraid to, just like Heather. I needed to talk to her, but I would have to wait until I got home to my computer. If only I could think about something else. I hurried back to the classroom just in time to hear Mrs. Patterlin give out our next assignment.

"Class, Heather will be just fine. And here's Gwendolyn. All right then, it's time for Language Arts. So get out your notebooks and get writing about your islands for awhile. This is also a writing and cursive lesson rolled into one. Please settle down and begin."

More than ever, I couldn't stand sitting next to Olivia. As we dug in our desks for our notebooks, she tipped her head toward me as she bent to look inside.

"Poor little Heather, huh Gwennie?"

"Shut up, Olivia. I know what you've been doing."

"Whatever are you talking about, Gwennie ?"

"You know very well what I'm talking about, Olivia, and, for your information, Heather has the note."

"What do you mean? I saw you give it to Andrew."

"You must be slipping, Olivia; that was ages ago. Heather has it now."

Olivia gripped my arm and dug in her nails. I did everything I could to pull away, but her grip grew stronger.

"Both of you had better keep your little mouths shut. That note proves nothing." She let go. I pulled my sweater down over my bruised arm.

Mrs. Patterlin, who had been working on a bulletin board during our conversation, was now heading in our direction.

"Why aren't you girls working?"

"I was just trying to help Gwen find her notebook, but we're all set now." Olivia oozed in her syrupy way.

"I'm glad to hear it. Now get to work." Mrs. Patterlin turned to go.

Maybe I could tell Mrs. Patterlin. I think she would believe me.

Just then Mrs. Patterlin turned back.

"Oh, by the way, girls, I have the results of the spelling test from Friday and I would like to talk to you about them later in the day."

"Oh, great," Olivia mouthed under her breath.

"Did you say something, Livi?"

"No, Mrs. Patterlin. I didn't say anything."

With all that had been going on, I had totally forgotten about the spelling test. I actually looked forward to our meeting with Mrs. Patterlin. The truth "would out" as they say in detective movies. Olivia just tucked her head in her notebook and lifted the side facing me so she could hide. It was fine by me. The less I saw of her face, the better. Although my mind was on Heather, I tried to focus on my writing. I flipped through my notebook and found where I had left off.

Oh, that's right; Heather and I were at the giant wheel.

"A couple of your friends are already aboard," Jonathon added.

"Oh, no," I thought. Would we have to deal with Olivia and Amanda so soon?

"Friends?"

"A couple of nice young fellows named Andrew and Hermy. They're at the top."

"Perfect. It'll be fun having them here," Heather said with a smile.

We strained our necks to look up to the top of the gigantic wheel.

"Hey, Andrew, Hermy, can you hear me? It's Gwen and Heather." I shouted as loudly as I could.

"Here, use my megaphone. I usually only use it in case of emergency, but I'll make an exception this time."

"Thanks, Jonathon. Andrew, Hermy, hello; it's Gwen and Heather!"

Leaning over the hand bar of the seat at the top of the wheel, Andrew and Hermy waved back.

"Hello down there! We'll talk to you after the ride!" Andrew shouted.

"Sounds good!"

Heather and I scrambled into the seat and Jonathon secured the latch. Up, up, up we glided to the peak of the wheel. Our stomachs tickled by the thrill flipped and made us giggle. At the top of the wheel, the whole park lay before us. The flume ride, the tilt-a-whirl, the carousel and more all spread out at our feet. Plus the flower gardens I had wished for covered the ground like an oriental rug. For a wonderful few minutes, we totally forgot about Olivia and Amanda. Andrew and Hermy would be great fun. We swooped around the wheel about ten times and then signaled to Jonathon that we wanted to get off. Our stomachs growled instead of giggled and we needed some food soon. We waited for the boys to get off.

"Thanks for the ride, Jonathon," I said. "I don't know about the rest of you, but I need food immediately."

"I'm always hungry," Hermy said grinning.

"I think I may starve to death," Andrew groaned as he pretended to swoon. We all laughed.

"Me too," Heather added. "I'm so glad that we didn't stop to eat the lunch that Olivia left for us."

"Good decision. She probably doused it with arsenic sprinkles," Andrew added.

"I wouldn't doubt it," Heather said with a shake of her head.

"What do you recommend, Jonathon?" I asked.

"Well, Gwen, there's a Delicious Delicacies stand around that grove of trees and an excellent Rainbow Candy Fluff cart across from it."

"Sounds good to me." Hermy smacked his lips. Everyone agreed.

"Jonathon, will we see you again?"

"Sure, Gwen. I do many tasks on your island. Plus, I will always be nearby if you need me."

It felt good to know that Jonathon would be around in case we needed help. We followed his directions and found "Delicious Delicacies." And who should the man behind the counter look like, but my Uncle Chops, the best chef in the world.

So far I loved my island. After enjoying savory turkey legs and a huge pitcher of fresh lemonade, we devoured absolutely the best rainbow fluff candy ever. Things could not be better. Just then out from the funhouse stepped . . . .

"Okay, class; it's time to put your notebooks and pens away and get ready for lunch. Girls from clusters 5 followed by 4 and so forth may get their lunches or lunch cards and line up. When all the girls have lined up, the boys may follow in the same order. Let's see if you can follow directions. Ready? Go."

"Mrs. Patterlin, will Heather be at lunch?" I needed to know.

"No, dear. Mrs. Muller sent her home for the remainder of the day."

I turned to Andrew.

"Hey, Andrew, do you mind if I eat with you and Hermy again today?"

"Of course not, Gwen."

"Of course not, Gwen." Olivia mimicked. "Aren't we the cute couple?"

"Just butt out, Olivia, and mind your own business," Andrew snapped back.

"You didn't seem to mind *your* business when you took my note."

"Hey, when you drop it on the floor, it becomes public property."

Olivia huffed off and grabbed her lunch from her cubby.

Andrew turned to me.

"It's too bad about Heather, huh?"

"Yes, and what until you hear what really happened."

Chapter 37
Info and Insult

Andrew's eyes widened. "You've got to be kidding me. Olivia thought that her ridiculous sign would destroy Heather's and my friendship? Yeah, like that would ever happen. We've been good friends for a long time. I'm just sorry that she tripped and fell. And that note. Olivia was stupid to put what she did in writing. You're right, Gwen. All the notes are evidence of her bullying. We can't afford to lose any of them."

Andrew's words told me what I had known all along. That he was definitely a good person to have as a friend. With his eyes bulging, Hermy listened and nodded.

"You've got to tell someone," Hermy spoke up, almost choking on his cheeseburger.

"Hermy's right. Things are definitely getting out of hand, Gwen. Maybe you and Heather should tell your parents or Mrs. Patterlin."

"I don't know, guys; I mean, what if they don't believe us and Olivia does something worse?"

"But she can't be allowed to get away with this stuff."

"I'm going to e-mail Heather tonight to see how she's feeling. Maybe she's thought of a plan. Plus, I'm going to remind her to pull Olivia's note out of her pocket before her mother sees it."

"Maybe the best thing would be if her mother did see it," Andrew said seriously.

"Hey, you two, enjoying your lunch?" Olivia slithered by with her crew. Amanda and the M&M's giggled.

Andrew spoke up.

"Why don't you and your fan club get lost?"

"Ah, Andrew, I didn't know you cared. Come on, girls. Good-bye, lovebirds."

"Hey, Olivia."

"Yes, Claire?"

"I'll see you later at our meeting with Mrs. Patterlin. It should be very interesting."

"Oh, why don't you just go back where you came from or, better yet, drop dead?" Olivia stormed off with the others close behind.

"What meeting with Mrs. Patterlin? Are you in trouble or something?"

"No, Hermy, I don't think so, but I think I know who is."

Chapter 38
Attempt to Avoid

I skipped the restroom because I didn't feel like running into Olivia. If I needed to go later, I'd just have to put up with Mrs. Patterlin's questioning why I didn't go at break. Olivia's bullying was affecting everything.

If only I didn't have to go out for recess. I knew that Olivia would be in my face again. I did have a sniffle; maybe that would be enough for Mrs. Patterlin to let me go to the library instead.

"Excuse me, Mrs. Patterlin, but I was just wondering."

"Yes, Gwendolyn?"

"Well, you see, I kind of have a sniffle and might be coming down with a cold and I was just wondering if I could stay in from recess today?"

"The school rule says that if you don't have a note from your mother or your doctor, then you must go out for recess. I'm sorry, Gwendolyn."

"Mrs. Patterlin, could you just this once make an exception?"

"No, dear; you know that I must abide by the school rules too."

"Yes, Mrs. Patterlin." I sadly turned to go.

"Gwendolyn?"

"Yes, Mrs. Patterlin?"

"Is there something bothering you, dear; I mean other than the sniffles?"

Here was my chance. But wasn't Olivia one of Mrs. Patterlin's favorites?

"No, Mrs. Patterlin. I'm fine."

"I'm glad to hear it. Oh, by the way, Gwendolyn, I called Heather's mom during lunch and she's doing much better."

"Thanks, Mrs. Patterlin."

Now *that* was good news. Dealing with Olivia would be a little easier now that I knew that Heather would be okay.

Chapter 39
A Regular Recess

As I exited the school and headed for the playground, I spotted Andrew and Hermy just ahead so I ran to catch up with them.

"Hey, guys. Could I hang out with you?"

"Sure, Gwen." Hermy's plump cheeks wiggled as he talked.

"So what's the scoop on the meeting with Mrs. Patterlin?"

"Well, Andrew, I don't know if you noticed or not, but Olivia was leaning way over in my direction during Friday's spelling test."

"I saw her." Hermy interrupted. "She was practically sitting on your chair."

"Yeah. I think she used a cheat sheet too," Andrew added.

"Right. Well, when she picked up the papers, Olivia also handed Mrs. Patterlin the cheat sheet saying she 'found' it near my desk."

"Unbelievable. Wait a minute. What am I saying? It's totally believable."

"Then what happened?" Hermy moved in closer.

"Well, as you know, Mrs. Patterlin gave us the test over again. It was kind of my idea. Anyway, I knew that I had nothing to lose and that the truth would come out."

"That was brilliant." Hermy added.

"So that's what the meeting is about."

I nodded.

"Of course, in addition to Heather's having Olivia's note, this spelling test thing has made her even more furious."

"Wow, I can't wait to watch Olivia's face during the meeting," Hermy said excitedly.

"Calm down, Hermy. We don't know exactly how things will turn out," Andrew urged.

"Right," I added.

"You know; it's funny."

"What's funny, Andrew?"

"Well, up through second grade Olivia wasn't a bad kid at all. If fact, she was kind of nice. I wonder what made her change."

"Heather seems to know her the best, but she hasn't told me yet what happened with Olivia back then."

"Well, whatever it was, it must have been pretty bad."

"Hey, come on; let's grab those three swings. We can't have recess go by without having a little fun." I ran ahead with the boys trailing behind.

Chapter 40
Chorus, Wonderful Chorus

Recess ended without a hitch. Olivia and the girls had to sit on the bench by the entrance to the school because they had wandered off too close to the wooded area, a definite no-no. So basically, Andrew, Hermy and I got to go wherever we wanted on the playground without having to run into the Foxfield Four. What a relief.

"Now, class, before we get ready for our next activity, would you all please place your language arts notebooks in the basket on my desk. I'd like to take a look at what you've been writing so far."

Wondering what Mrs. Patterlin would think about my writing, I dug out my notebook and placed it in the basket. Then I thought about Heather's notebook.

"Mrs. Patterlin, would you like me to check to see if Heather's notebook is in her desk?"

"Yes, please, Gwendolyn."

Neatly placed on her pile of books lay Heather's new language arts notebook. I put hers on top of mine in the basket.

"Chorus members may now line up at the door."

Chorus? My hand immediately flew into the air.

"Yes, Gwen?"

"Mrs. Patterlin, I'd love to join chorus. Do I have to audition or anything?"

"No, dear, it's open to anyone who enjoys singing. If that's you, please line up now."

I was sure that Heather was in chorus too.

"Those of you who are not signed up for chorus, please line up at the back of the line. You will help me accompany the chorus members to Mrs. Ray's room."

I noticed that the Foxfield Four stood at the back of the line. On my way to lining up, I overheard Olivia whispering to Amanda.

"Chorus is for nerds. It's stupid and a waste of time."

"I don't know," Amanda answered. "I really used to like it. I loved singing in the holiday and spring concerts. Mom and Dad enjoyed seeing me on the stage too."

"Don't be lame. Only geeks like to do stuff like that."

I couldn't hold back.

"Amanda, Olivia is wrong. Chorus *is* fun and, with a cool teacher like Mrs. Ray, it must be wonderful. I'm sure that you can still join."

"Gwen, just shut up."

"I won't shut up. Amanda has a mind of her own and if she wants to be in chorus it's her choice and not yours. You're not anyone's boss."

Amanda looked at me with a very sad look in her eyes. Obviously, Olivia's bullying never stopped, even in her own group of so-called friends.

"All right, Amanda; if you want to, go ahead and join the chorus geeks, but don't expect to stay my friend."

Amanda held her head down and answered, "Forget what I said, Olivia; you're right. Chorus is for nerds."

"Now you're talking smart. We can just hang out while the birdies sing their stupid songs."

I tried again. "Remember, Amanda, you can always change your mind. Don't let Olivia bully you."

"Sorry, Gwen." Amanda looked even sadder, if that were possible.

Olivia glared at me and pushed Amanda back behind her in line.

"I've had just about enough of you, Claire. Watch yourself."

Olivia's hateful glare plunged into me like a sharp dagger. Chorus couldn't come soon enough.

Mrs. Ray welcomed me and told me that I would be standing next to Heather on the risers. It took a while for me to get used to it all mainly because the group was about three sessions ahead of me, but I just love music so I didn't mind one bit. Time just flew by.

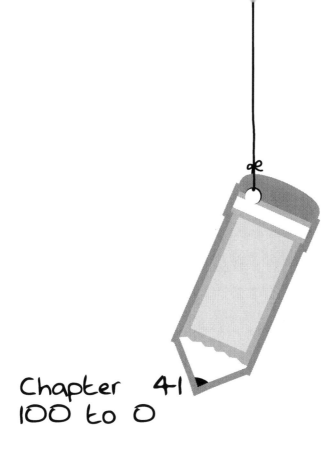

Chapter 41
100 to 0

"On your desk, class, you will find another copy of this week's spelling words. As you can see, they are not in alphabetical order. Your job is to put them in order on the front of your paper and then to write each word five times correctly in your best cursive on the back. Remember: if you spell them five times incorrectly, then you will have to write them correctly ten times. So be careful. You may begin."

After a bit of rustling around, we all began the ABC process. A comfortable silence filled the room until Mrs. Patterlin spoke again in a much quieter voice than before.

"Gwendolyn and Olivia, may I see you please?"

The spelling test.

Standing with our backs to the class, we faced Mrs. Patterlin.

"I have corrected your tests, girls, and I know which of you did not take the test honestly. If either of you has anything to say, please do so now."

I knew that even though the other kids' eyes were looking down on their papers that their ears were straining to hear every word that Mrs. Patterlin said. Olivia, surprisingly, spoke first.

"I took it honestly, Mrs. Patterlin. Cheating is wrong. I found the cheat sheet right next to Gwen's desk."

"Yes, it is true that cheating is wrong. And it may be that the cheat sheet was right next to Gwen's desk. However, you, Olivia, did not take the test honestly."

Olivia turned white.

"You see, Olivia, when I gave the two of you the test over again, I mixed up "their, there, and they're" and gave them to you differently than on the first test. On the first test both you and Gwen spelled the correct form of each word in the correct order, but on the retest, you did not."

"But, I . . . ."

"There are no excuses for such behavior, Olivia. Not only did you cheat on the test, but also you suggested that Gwen had and now you have lied to me. Unfortunately, it will be necessary for me to call your mother tonight."

I felt weird inside. I mean I was glad that Olivia had been caught and that I had been found innocent of cheating, but I also felt sorry in a way for Olivia. I don't know why; I just did.

"Here are your tests. Due to your cheating, Olivia, you received a zero. You know that there is a zero tolerance policy for cheating in my classroom."

I looked down at my 100 and folded the paper in half.

"You may now go back to your desks and continue your spelling work with the rest of the class."

As we took our seats, I glanced at Andrew who gave me a secretive thumbs-up. I smiled a weak smile. With tears flowing down her face,

Olivia scratched a few words on the back of her spelling test and then lifted it for me to see.

"I hate you, Gwendolyn Claire."

I looked into Olivia's eyes and felt sadness for her, but I couldn't ignore her words.

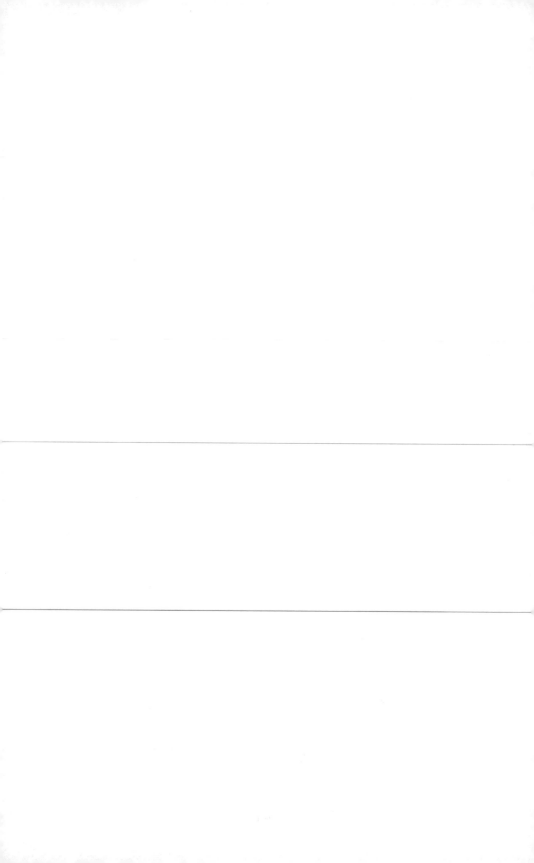

Chapter 42
Island Intrigue

Mrs. Patterlin's words broke the silence as the clock read exactly 3:00 p.m.

"If you have not finished your spelling, please do so for homework. Now before we begin getting ready for dismissal, I would like to return your language arts notebooks to you."

Walking among us while passing out the notebooks, Mrs. Patterlin continued to talk. "I must admit that most of you are working hard on your writing. However . . ."

Mrs. Patterlin neared Benny.

"Some of you must put in a little more effort."

She neared me and held out my notebook.

"Others of you are very creative and have wild imaginations."

Mrs. Patterlin leaned over and whispered in my ear.

"Gwen, please read my note to you at the end of your writing. Not now, but later when you get home."

Mrs. Patterlin's comment made me a little nervous.

"You will notice that I have put a letter grade at the end of your writing. For homework tonight I expect you to write for at least fifteen minutes. Remember: use your imagination and have fun."

By this time Mrs. Patterlin had passed out all the notebooks.

"Line leaders, please distribute the daily notes. The rest of you may get ready for dismissal."

Emily handed me my note. A shiny blue star met my eyes. Whew. A positive daily note is a good way to end the day.

Olivia grabbed her note, looked at it, crumpled it up, and stuffed it in her backpack.

Chapter 43
Not Exactly the Truth

"Hard day, Gwen?"

"Exhausting day, Mom."

"Exhausting day, how?"

"It's just that so many things happened."

I filled Mom in on Heather's getting hurt and having to go home, but I didn't include anything about Olivia's part in it. In fact I didn't mention Olivia at all except for the part about the spelling test.

"Wow, that was an exhausting day. Mine was pretty hectic too."

"I did get a star on my daily note."

"That's my girl."

"And I joined chorus."

"Great."

"And Mrs. Ray, my music teacher, teaches piano and has an opening at the same time as Heather's lesson."

"Let's sign you up."

"I was hoping you'd say that, Mom. Mrs. Ray is going to call you tonight."

"Wow, it *was* a busy day. I could go for a coffee right about now. Would you like a hot chocolate?"

"Sounds great, Mom."

We stopped at a donut shop drive-through and then headed for home.

As I sipped my hot chocolate, I stared out the window and just let my mind drift. That didn't last for long because suddenly I remembered Mrs. Patterlin's note. I thought that she would like my writing, but maybe she didn't. Then again maybe her note wasn't about my writing at all.

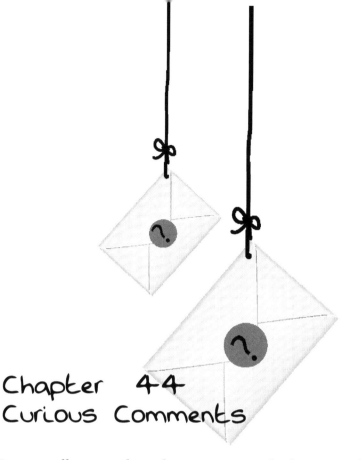

Chapter 44
Curious Comments

I practically tripped up the stairs as I rushed to read the note from Mrs. Patterlin.

"What's the hurry, honey?"

"Nothing, Mom. I just can't wait to change my clothes and get my homework done."

"Okay. I'll call you when it's time to set the table."

"Alright."

I didn't *really* lie to Mom. I mean I really couldn't wait to get on my sweats and finish my homework.

Flipping through my notebook, I noticed some comments on the pages, but I decided to read them later. The note. Where was the note? I turned to the last page of my writing to find Mrs. Patterlin's perfect teacher handwriting. I was almost afraid to read it.

A+ Your writing is excellent and you use your imagination well;

So far, so good.

However, I am concerned about the content of your writing.

I am also concerned about the content of Heather's writing.

I would like to meet with both of you tomorrow.

You have done nothing wrong, Gwen. Mrs. Patterlin

Now I was worried. What concerned Mrs. Patterlin about my content? I decided to e-mail Heather immediately. Mrs. Patterlin was concerned about Heather's content too. What did *she* write about? Yikes.

From: *gwenclaire@scribble2me.com*
Reply to: *gwenclaire@scribble2me.com*
To: *heathers@penme.net*
Subject: How are you and stuff

Hi, Heather. How you are doing? Olivia is definitely taking
this bullying thing too far. I haven't told my mom or anyone.
Have you? Andrew and Hermy think we should. Any ideas?
Another thing: Mrs. Patterlin collected our language arts notebooks
today and put this note at the end of my writing. [I included the note
here.]
What do you think it all means?
Write back. Gwen

I hit the "Send" button, hoping that Heather would e-mail me back quickly. I decided to look over Mrs. Patterlin's comments. Most of them were pretty ordinary teacher comments until I turned to where Heather was really upset that I had invited Olivia and Amanda to the island. How could I have been so stupid? I knew that Mrs. Patterlin would read the notebooks someday. She had drawn an arrow to this part and written: "Is there a problem?" A little further along, she had put a question mark next to the words "Foxfield Four."

I stared at my computer screen waiting for a message from Heather.

Chapter 45
Lies, E-mails, and a Phone Call

"Gwen, I thought that you liked grilled cheese sandwiches and tomato soup."

"I do."

"Well, you've only eaten part of your sandwich and you've hardly touched your soup."

"Sorry, Mom. I guess I'm just not that hungry."

"Is something wrong, Honey? You're usually starving by now."

"Nothing's wrong, Mom. Maybe the hot chocolate spoiled my appetite."

I hated lying to Mom, but I was scared that if I told her what was bothering me, she would call Mrs. Patterlin. If I could speak to Mrs. Patterlin in private, maybe I could give her an explanation that she would accept.

"That's hard to believe, Gwen, but I know that you never lie to me."

Now I felt even worse. I needed to leave the table before I broke into tears.

"May I please be excused, Mom?"

"Sure, dear; I'll check in on you in a few minutes."

I turned to bring my dish to the sink.

"Just a minute, honey; what's that bruise on your arm?"

"Oh, it's nothing, Mom."

"Let me see it." I moved closer. "It looks like someone squeezed your arm really hard."

"It must have happened when we were playing tag during recess. It doesn't hurt, Mom, really. I'd forgotten all about it."

Mom looked me straight in the eye and I'm not sure that she believed me.

"Okay, if you're sure you're alright. You *are* telling me the whole truth, aren't you, Gwen?"

"Of course, Mom." I could barely get out the words.

"Alright then; scoot," Mom gave me a quick kiss and a pat on the behind.

I bounded up the stairs. Things were getting worse. I was lying to Mom. I clicked on my computer. There was an e-mail from Heather.

From: *heathers@penme.net*
Reply to: *heathers@penme.net*
To: *gwenclaire@scribble2me.com*
Subject: RE: How are you and stuff

I'm still here. My knees are sore but my stomach's okay. My parents always get so upset when anything happens to me and I keep lying to them about what's been going on. Plus, I think I understand what Mrs. Patterlin's note means. This whole mess with Olivia bothered me so much that I couldn't even concentrate on the island project after my notebook was stolen. I just kept doodling in it and using it to write down some of the stuff that was happening. I didn't mention Olivia's name though, but I did use initials like O and FF. I didn't think that Mrs. Patterlin would collect the notebooks so soon without telling us a day in advance. I thought that I would just do the real assignment at the last minute. I wasn't thinking. As far as ideas go, I have none. Write back. H.

P.S. I begged Mom to go to piano tonight and she finally agreed; piano always makes me feel better. I'm leaving in a few minutes.

From: *gwenclaire@scribble2me.com*
Reply to: *gwenclaire@scribble2me.com*
To: *heathers@penme.net*
Subject: Back to you

How can either of us think straight? It's so hard to concentrate on school work when we're constantly dealing with the Foxfield Four. I've been lying to my mom too. Olivia grabbed my arm today and made marks on it; Mom, of course, noticed them and I lied to her about how I got them.

I wonder when Mrs. Patterlin will talk to us. What a mess!

Try to have fun at piano. See you tomorrow. Gwen

I hit the "Send" button. Just then I heard Mom calling.

"Gwen, Mrs. Ray is on the phone and would like to talk with you. Could you come down please?"

"Coming, Mom." Mrs. Ray wanted to talk to me?

When I entered the kitchen, Mom smiled and handed me the receiver.

"Hello?"

"Hi, Gwen. It's Mrs. Ray. How are you tonight?"

"Fine, thank you."

"Good. I was just wondering what you were doing in about twenty minutes."

"Um, just homework or reading, I guess." I looked questioningly at Mom.

"Well, your mom and I were just talking about lessons for you and I wondered if you would like to join Heather for a lesson this evening?"

"That would be great." I again glanced up at Mom's smiling face.

"Fantastic. Bring some of the music that you were working on with your last piano teacher. I'll be seeing you soon. Bye."

"See you soon. Bye."

I jumped up to hug Mom.

"Thanks, Mom."

"Well, what are we waiting for? Let's get going. I have the directions to Mrs. Ray's house and she's not too far from here."

I grabbed my music tote from the top of the piano and threw my jacket over my shoulders. Mrs. Ray was so much fun and I couldn't wait to start piano again.

"Boy, will Heather ever be surprised. Hey, you'll get to meet Mrs. Ray *and* Heather."

"Sounds perfect."

We hurried to the car and I thought how wonderful it would be to see Heather away from school and the Foxfield Four.

Chapter 46
Mrs. Ray's Duo

Mrs. Ray lived in a huge Victorian house up a long driveway on the top of a hill. Mom and I parked in front, climbed the stairs of the wrap-around porch and rang the doorbell. There was only one other car in the driveway so I guessed that Heather wasn't here yet.

The polished wood door opened.

"Well, hello, Gwen. And this must be Mrs. Claire. Come in please."

Ahead of us a curved wide staircase led upstairs. To our right the most beautiful room I had ever seen glowed in the light of the fireplace and in that room stood two pianos placed side by side.

"Heather should be here momentarily. Her mom just called to say that they were running a little late."

"Gwen has been looking forward to continuing her piano lessons, Mrs. Ray. It is so nice of you to take her on as your student."

"The pleasure is all mine. I see that you've brought your music."

"Yes, Mrs. Ray. These are the pieces that I played for my recital last year."

"I see. These are challenging arrangements and I am pleased to say that Heather and you appear to be on the same level. That will make things much easier."

Just then the doorbell rang.

Mrs. Ray answered the door and in stepped Heather and her mom. Heather's eyes widened and her mouth dropped open.

"Gwen, are you here for lessons too? Why didn't you tell me?"

"I didn't find out myself until about fifteen minutes ago."

I ran to Heather. In spite of her aching knees, we jumped up and down in a circle. In the meantime Mrs. Ray introduced Mom to Mrs. Sebastian.

"Mrs. Claire, would you like to go out for coffee while the girls have their lessons?"

"That sounds like a wonderful idea, Mrs. Sebastian."

"All right, then. Let's go. I know a fantastic coffee shop just down the street that has the most delicious pastries. Work hard and have fun, girls. Bye for now."

Heather and I sat down at the pianos. My stomach quivered with excitement.

Chapter 47
A Chance to Talk

After we had played several warm-ups, Mrs. Ray asked us to play "Fur Elise" by Beethoven. She gave us copies of the same arrangement. I loved the piece and had played it at recital. Heather had actually played it at the spring concert in 4th grade. I had never played a duet with anyone before and to play one with Heather was the coolest thing in the world. At first we made mistakes. Well, actually, most of the mistakes were mine; the arrangement was a little different from the one I had used in recital. We had to start over a few times, but once we relaxed and got going it sounded really beautiful.

"Brava, ladies. Brava."

Mrs. Ray stood and applauded as we grinned like silly four year olds.

"You two play just beautifully together. I can't wait for us to begin the study of a new piece that you can learn together."

Heather and I couldn't stop smiling. This had been the best part of the whole day. Why couldn't school feel this way? We loved being here and we were learning something new. Mrs. Ray was our teacher and this was our "piano school." It was safe here. That was the difference. It didn't feel safe at Foxfield School, not with bullies like Olivia around.

After we had played for another fifteen minutes or so, Mrs. Ray asked if we would like a snack. Since I hadn't eaten that much for supper, I said, "yes" perhaps a little too enthusiastically.

"Okay, then. Why don't you girls relax for a few minutes and I'll be right back with some refreshments." Mrs. Ray walked down the hallway that led to the kitchen at the back of her home.

I spoke first.

"I'm so glad that we have a chance to talk."

"Me too. Gwen, this Foxfield Four thing makes me not want to go to school."

"I know. If it weren't for you, I wouldn't want to go either. Why is Olivia so mean?"

"It started in second grade. That year Olivia's dad left her and her mom. My mom didn't tell me much about it. She only said that Olivia's mom and dad did not get along. One day he left home and they haven't heard from him since. That was almost three years ago."

"I know how it feels not to have a dad. It's not easy."

"Olivia started getting bad grades, and she was sent to the principal's office a lot."

"So what happened between the two of you?"

"Well, my parents heard about the trouble Olivia was getting in and decided that I shouldn't play with her anymore. They didn't want me to get into trouble too."

"That must have really hurt Olivia and gotten her mad too."

"It did. And whenever I've tried to make a new friend, she's gotten really nasty."

"So this has been going on for a long time already."

"Yes, but as we get older, Olivia gets meaner."

"I can feel sorry for her, in a way; but she's really become a bully."

"I know."

"Why do Amanda and the M&M's stay with her?"

"I think they're scared of her."

"She definitely can be scary."

Heather nodded.

"Rather than fight, they stay her so-called 'friends.'"

"Today Amanda seemed to want to rejoin chorus, but Olivia made her feel that only nerds were in chorus."

"I remember when Olivia quit chorus. Soon after she did, Amanda did too. It's sad because they both have really nice voices."

"And the M&M's?"

"Olivia convinced them to quit too."

"That's too bad."

"Mom and Olivia's mother used to be friends too. When Olivia's dad left, her mom stopped calling. Now my mother thinks that Olivia's mom is trying to make good changes in her life and that's why she ran for P.T.G. president last spring."

"If only Olivia would change."

"I know. Gwen, I'm really nervous about our meeting with Mrs. Patterlin."

"So am I. She's going to ask a lot of questions."

"Should we tell her what's been going on with Olivia?"

"What about Olivia?"

There stood Mrs. Ray with a tray filled with chocolate milk and cookies.

Heather and I just looked at each other. I felt my throat dry up and my tongue stick to the roof of my mouth. I swallowed hard.

"You both look so serious, girls. Is there something wrong?"

The house echoed the sound of the ticking clock in the hall. Neither of us spoke.

Chapter 48
Our Chance

"If you two have a problem, would you like to talk about it? After all, Olivia is my student too. Maybe I can help."

Now was our chance to tell an adult, a wonderful adult that we trusted.

"No, Mrs. Ray, there's nothing wrong," I barely squeezed the words out of my mouth.

"Oh, it's nothing, Mrs. Ray," Heather jumped in. "Since Gwen is new to Foxfield, I was just telling her some things about the kids in our class."

"That's right, Mrs. Ray.It's hard being the new kid especially in fifth grade when most of the other kids have known each other since Kindergarten. So Heather was just filling me in a little."

"Are you girls sure that's all it is? Remember: you can always come to me or any other teacher at school if you are having a problem."

"There's no problem, Mrs. Ray," Heather answered.

We were lying again. Why didn't we tell Mrs. Ray the truth right now? Would we lie to Mrs. Patterlin too?

"Okay, ladies, if you say so. Now let's have some milk and homemade oatmeal raisin cookies. You do like oatmeal raisin, I hope."

Even though I had again lost my appetite, I managed to down a few cookies and a glass of milk. Heather did the same. Unfortunately, the rest of the lesson didn't feel quite the same. We had lied to Mrs. Ray, one of the nicest teachers at Foxfield. Olivia's bullying had reared its ugly head again.

Chapter 49
The "Nightmare"

I tossed and turned most of the night. I kept seeing Olivia's face and the rest of the Foxfield Four grinning at me like hungry hyenas. Then I kept going over and over the lies that I had told to Mom and Mrs. Ray. My brain kept spinning around and around wondering what Mrs. Patterlin would ask us the next day. Just as I had finally dozed off, I heard Mom's voice.

"Honey, time to get up. How do waffles sound?"

Mom was softly pushing the hair off my forehead. I looked up into her kind eyes and the tears started streaming down my face.

"Oh, Mom," I choked on my words.

"What's the matter, Honey?"

Oh, how I wanted to tell her what was happening at school, but then I lied again.

"I just had the worst dream." I hugged Mom as hard as I could. "I dreamt that there were these monsters who had taken over Foxfield. They bossed everyone. Plus they loved hurting and picking on people. No matter how I tried, I couldn't seem to get them to leave my friends and me alone. No matter how fast we ran from them, they were always there."

"It sounds like your monsters are the kind that often exists in schools. We used to call them bullies when I went to school and I'm sure that they're still called that today. I got bullied quite a bit."

"You did? Really, Mom?"

"Absolutely. There was this group of girls who already wore make-up in 6th grade and would pick on me during bathroom break. I was small for my age and, of course, even if I had been bigger, Grammie would never have let me wear make-up. Even when I was in high school, I had to beg to wear a little lipstick." Mom smiled and looked at her watch.

"What did they do to you, Mom?"

"Look, Honey, it's getting late and we'd better get moving. Take a quick shower and get dressed. I'll get the waffles going and I promise I'll tell you the whole story on the way to school."

"Okay, Mom." I jumped out of bed and headed for my bathroom.

"Gwen, you aren't being bullied at school, are you?"

"It was just a nightmare, Mom." I quickly got out of that situation and into the hot shower.

Chapter 50
Flashback

"They actually locked the bathroom stall doors?"

"Yes, do you believe it? Barbara and Robin would rush ahead of Linda, my best friend, and me to the girls' room, go in each stall, lock it and slide out from under the doors. By the time we got there, they were putting on makeup at the mirror. We tried each stall door and obviously couldn't get in. We weren't about to look under the stall doors or climb under for that matter. They just stood there laughing at us."

"What did you do?"

"Nothing at first. We just let them get away with it. We tried to get to the bathroom during lunch and not the usual break time, but that wasn't always easy."

"Didn't it make you mad?"

"You bet it did. Finally they started doing other things like tearing our homework as we passed it down the row to our teacher, stuff like that."

"What did you do?"

"Well, we put up with it for a long time until one day when things really got out of hand. While coming back from the library on the third floor, Robin shoved Linda who was at the head of the line and she fell down a flight of stairs. Linda was out of school for a week after that. Robin had been so secretive about the whole thing that no one suspected anything. When Linda came back to school, she told me that Robin had pushed her. That was when we told our homeroom teacher what had been happening."

"Weren't you afraid that they'd do something even worse?"

"Of course we were afraid, but we decided that the bravest thing to do was to stand up to them, not alone of course, but with the support of adults we trusted. Linda could have been killed in that fall. Telling on someone who is trying to hurt you is not tattle-taling."

By the time Mom had finished her story, we were pulling up to the front door of the school. Mom had given me lots to think about.

"Thanks for telling me about what happened to you, Mom. I'll see you after school. Love you."

"Love you, too. Just remember, Gwen, going to school should not be scary. You should always feel safe while you're there. There are always people ready to help you keep safe. See you soon."

I scurried up the stairs and down the hall to my room. Classes had already started. It seems that Mom and I had ended up running a little later than usual. I hurried to my seat and noticed that Olivia's seat was empty.

Chapter 51
Track "Meet"

Amanda was missing too. I can't say that I was disappointed to have half of the Foxfield Four absent. The M&M's didn't really do anything on their own; they were just followers. I looked forward to a peaceful day.

"Class, I expect that you have almost completed your morning work. You may finish during break. Right now let's line up for gym. Girls from all clusters may line up first."

I grabbed my gym gear and hurried to line up behind Heather.

"I wonder where Olivia and Amanda are."

"I don't know, Gwen, but I do know one thing."

"What's that?"

"I don't miss them."

"Me either. Heather, there's something I need to tell you during gym. We're still running track, right?"

"I think so. My knees still hurt, so I'll be running a little more slowly today."

"My knees aren't that perfect yet either. I don't think that Mr. Santini will mind if we take it a little slower today. Then we'll have a chance to talk. My mom told me a very interesting story on the way to school."

"Okay, class. Let's get moving."

Mr. Santini greeted us at the gym door with his huge smile.

"Good morning, class. Today you will be doing one of your favorite gym activities, running track."

Groans echoed from the class. Heather and I, of course, were happy. Mrs. Patterlin stepped forward and spoke something in Mr. Santini's ear.

"Oh, I'm so happy that you are pleased with today's activity. Heather and Gwen, could you step out of line for a moment please? The rest of you, get going. Head out through the far doors and start your laps. See you in a little while, you two."

We watched as our class disappeared out the door. Mrs. Patterlin leaned down.

"Ladies, I'll only keep you a moment. I just wanted to let you know that we'll be having our meeting at the end of the school day. Don't worry; everything will be fine. You are not in trouble. Now go catch up with the class." Mrs. Patterlin smiled after us as we hurried out to the track.

"Okay, so we know when our meeting is and we know we're not in trouble. The problem is what to tell Mrs. Patterlin." Heather looked concerned.

"Heather, after Mom told me a story about when she was in school, I kind of came up with a decision about what we should do. Come on, let's go. I'll tell you everything."

Chapter 52
The Decision

We started out trying to run slowly, but Heather's knees changed our plans.

"Ouch. Gwen, I think that walking around the track is all I can handle right now."

"That's okay. Mr. Santini just signaled us that we could slow down."

"So your mom was bullied too, huh?"

"Yes, and look what almost happened to her friend Linda. I couldn't take it if something bad like that happened to you."

"Or to you. Olivia just *might* try really hurting one of us. So you think that we should tell Mrs. Patterlin what's been happening?"

"Yes. I mean she's already suspicious that something is going on. Look what she wrote in our notebooks."

"That's true. Even though I'm a little bit scared about the whole thing right now, I think that we'll feel better once we tell someone."

"Andrew and Hermy even said that we should tell someone, remember?"

"That's right, they did."

"Okay, let's do it. We'll tell Mrs. Patterlin everything."

We high-fived and continued around the track. I didn't know about Heather, but I felt better already.

Chapter 53
The Meeting

At the end of the day while the rest of our class was watching a video with Mrs. Mendez's class, we would meet with Mrs. Patterlin. The afternoon actually went quicker than I thought it would.

"Class, as I promised, you will be viewing a special fun video in Mrs. Mendez's classroom today. I would like the boys to take their chairs and line up single file at the door. Girls, you may do the same once the boys have all left. Mrs. Mendez will direct you where to sit."

Mrs. Patterlin met our eyes and signaled us to stay put. Mrs. Mendez's door shut behind our class and Heather and I were alone with Mrs. Patterlin.

"Come have a seat at the big table, girls."

Mrs. Patterlin sat at the head of the table and we sat at either side of her.

"First of all, I will again emphasize that neither of you is in trouble with me. However, I do believe that you are experiencing some trouble here at Foxfield."

Mrs. Patterlin looked us both in the eye, first Heather and then me.

"Yes, Mrs. Patterlin," I said quietly.

"That's right, Mrs. Patterlin," Heather added.

"Would you like to tell me about it?"

We both nodded.

"Let's begin then."

Heather and I told Mrs. Patterlin about everything that had happened during the past several days. Heather had more to add because she had known Olivia for so long. Mrs. Patterlin patiently listened and took notes while we talked. We just talked and talked. After about twenty minutes or so, Mrs. Patterlin excused herself and went to the phone. Heather and I looked at each other and, almost on cue, breathed a deep sigh of relief.

"Hello, yes. Yes, we are finished. Okay, then. I'll be here." Mrs. Patterlin hung up the phone and returned to us. "Heather and Gwen, thank you for being brave enough to talk to me so openly about what has been happening. You may now join your classmates in Mrs. Mendez's room. Take your chairs."

As we left the room, we noticed Mrs. Ray; Mrs. Baxter; and Mr. Lawrence, the school principal, heading down our hall. The door to Mrs. Mendez's room closed behind us and we joined the world of "Hattie and the Haunted Cave." I couldn't help but wonder if another meeting was now going on in room 25.

Chapter 54
Mom?

"Mom, what are you doing here?" There stood Mom waiting outside our room after the video. The rest of the class filed passed us.

"What kind of a welcome is that?" Mom smiled and gave me a hug.

"I'm just surprised; that's all."

I looked over to see Heather talking with her parents too. Mr. and Mrs. Sebastian walked over to us.

"Gwen and Mom, would you like to join us for a cook-out at our house tonight?"

"That sounds lovely, Mr. Sebastian. What do you think, Gwen?"

"Sure, but . . . ."

"Okay, kids, why don't you grab your stuff and we'll get going. Mrs. Patterlin already knows that you are leaving a little early. Mrs. Claire, you can follow us."

"But, what's going on?" asked Heather.

"Don't worry, Heathie; we'll fill you in on the way home," answered Mrs. Sebastian.

Chapter 55
Behind the Scenes

Adults are sneaky. That's one conclusion that I came to after all was said and done. Here's what was happening behind the scenes at Foxfield Elementary.

Olivia and Amanda were not actually absent from school. They were in Mr. Lawrence's office all day, even for lunch. After school yesterday Mrs. Patterlin reported what she had discovered in our notebooks to Mr. Lawrence after she had spoken to our special area teachers who told her that they thought something was going on between the Foxfield Four and us too. Mr. Lawrence met with Olivia, Amanda, and their parents this morning. After our meeting with Mrs. Patterlin, she met with our teachers and Mr. Lawrence; but this time our parents attended too. Mom said that she and the Sebastians stayed hidden until we were safely in Mrs. Mendez's room.

Heather and I don't really know much else except that Olivia and Amanda got into deep trouble for their bullying. Things have been a lot more peaceful at Foxfield Elementary. Mrs. Patterlin had Heather and Olivia trade clusters so now Heather is with Andrew and me. It would really be cool if Hermy could join us too; well, maybe later in the school year.

We finally finished our island projects too. Mrs. Patterlin gave Heather extra time to finish hers. Olivia and the rest of the Foxfield Four haven't exactly been perfect, but they're acting much better. Olivia is even trying to be friendly. She actually gave me a new turquoise gel pen to use to finish my project. By the way, here's how "Gwendolyn's Island" turned out. Yes, I finally did come up with a name for it; it's nothing flashy, but it works.

So far I loved Gwendolyn's Island. After enjoying savory turkey legs and a huge pitcher of fresh lemonade, we devoured absolutely the best rainbow fluff candy ever. Things could not be better. Just then out from the funhouse stepped Olivia and Amanda looking like they had just seen a ghost.

"What happened to you two? You look as white as sheets," Andrew said.

Olivia ignored Andrew and walked straight up to me.

"Gwendolyn, what kind of an amusement park is this anyway? That funhouse was definitely not fun. I think that I may throw up."

"Me too." Amanda stood shaking next to Olivia.

"What do you mean?" Not having been in the funhouse yet, I thought that it would end up being just about like any other funhouse, filled with mirrors and twists and turns and crooked floors and actually not very scary at all.

"First the door slammed and locked behind us. It looked just like Foxfield Elementary at first."

"The funhouse looked like Foxfield Elementary?"

"Exactly like Foxfield." Amanda managed to squeak out.

"Well, I guess that anything's possible."

Heather moved closer.

"What was so scary about its looking like Foxfield?" I asked.

"Looking like Foxfield was weird but not scary. What happened in the halls was scary."

"What happened?"

"There were these girls,"Amanda started and Olivia interrupted.

"Yes, there were these girls, I mean they looked ordinary, but when we tried to walk past them, they shoved us into the wall and said horrible things to us, mean frightening things."

"I even got pushed into a girls' room and locked in a stall."

"I could hear Amanda screaming down the hall. Luckily I managed to get away from one of the girls and rescue her. They even stole our bags."

"Stole your bags?" Heather's eyes were as big as saucers.

"They threw our papers around like confetti and ripped up our notebooks, sheet by sheet." Amanda nervously kept pulling on her hair until I thought she would pull it out.

"The more we ran, the more they chased us. Their voices became louder and louder and sounded as if they were coming out of deep caves. They called us names and told us they would hurt us if we did not do what they wanted us to do."

"What did they want you to do?"

"I don't know. I just know that I wanted us to get out of there as quickly as we could."

"It was a nightmare." Amanda started to cry.

Heather stepped up and stood face to face with Olivia.

"It's funny, Olivia, but what you felt in the funhouse is what I feel everyday when I go to Foxfield Elementary. And you are correct; it's not fun. Did the girls in the funhouse remind you of anyone?"

"No, not really . . ."

"Olivia, think again. Didn't they remind you of anyone?"

"They remind me of us, Olivia, you and me, and how we have treated Heather."
Olivia looked over at Amanda.

"Well, Olivia, is Amanda right?"

"Yes."

"How did it feel?"

"Horrible."

"It sounds to me like those girls in the funhouse and the Foxfield Four have something in common."

"What's that?" Olivia looked down at her shoes.

"They are all bullies."

"Are we really that horrible to you, Heather?" Olivia was crying.

"Yes, Olivia. You are."

"I am so sorry." Olivia raised her eyes.

"I'm sorry too," Amanda added.

"Can you forgive me?"

"Not yet, but maybe someday, Olivia."

"We used to be such good friends."

"I know," Heather answered.

I stood there realizing that we were having a really grown-up moment. Then I noticed two leather bags on a bench behind Olivia and Amanda.

"Are those yours?" I said, pointing to the bags.

"Yes!" Olivia shouted. "How did they get there?"

"Well, the island is magical, remember."

"I was just thinking. What if we all go for a swim? We could stop at the swim shop over by the pond and pick out some suits and towels?"

"You mean you are asking Amanda and me to go swimming with all of you?"

"What do you think, Heather?" After all, it really was up to Heather. I wouldn't blame her for not wanting to be around Olivia.

"Sure, let's go."

"Alright then. Swimming it is."

The summer flew by and the amusement park disappeared as fast as it had appeared. The new school year began. Heather and Olivia are not what you would call "friends" yet, but who knows?

It had been a magical summer on Gwendolyn's Island and the greatest magic was what had happened at the funhouse that very first day.

The End